Lynne Graham

ROCCANTI'S MARRIAGE REVENGE

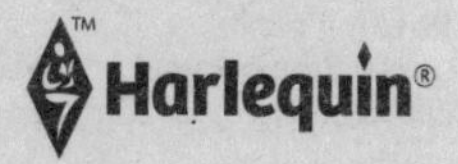

TORONTO NEW YORK LONDON
AMSTERDAM PARIS SYDNEY HAMBURG
STOCKHOLM ATHENS TOKYO MILAN MADRID
PRAGUE WARSAW BUDAPEST AUCKLAND

Recycling programs
for this product may
not exist in your area.

ISBN-13: 978-0-373-13061-0

ROCCANTI'S MARRIAGE REVENGE

This edition published by arrangement with Harlequin Books S.A.

For questions and comments about the quality of this book please contact us at Customer_eCare@Harlequin.ca.

www.Harlequin.com

Printed in U.S.A.

All about the author...
Lynne Graham

Of Irish/Scottish parentage, **LYNNE GRAHAM** has lived in Northern Ireland all her life. She has one brother. She grew up in a seaside village and now lives in a country house surrounded by a woodland garden, which is wonderfully private.

Lynne met her husband when she was fourteen; they married after she completed a degree at Edinburgh University. Lynne wrote her first book at fifteen—it was rejected everywhere. She started writing again when she was home with her first child. It took several attempts before she was published, and she has never forgotten the delight of seeing that book for sale at the local newsagents.

Lynne always wanted a large family, and she now has five children. Her eldest, her only natural child, is in her twenties and is a university graduate. Her other children, who are every bit as dear to her heart, are adopted: two from Sri Lanka and two from Guatemala. In Lynne's home, there is a rich and diverse cultural mix, which adds a whole extra dimension of interest and discovery to family life.

The family has two pets. Thomas, a very large and affectionate black cat, bosses the dog and hunts rabbits. The dog is Daisy, an adorable but not very bright West Highland white terrier, who loves being chased by the cat. At night, the dog and cat sleep together in front of the kitchen stove.

Lynne loves gardening and cooking, collects everything from old toys to rock specimens and is crazy about every aspect of Christmas.

Other titles by Lynne Graham available in eBook:

Harlequin Presents®

3025—JEWEL IN HIS CROWN
3011—THE MARRIAGE BETRAYAL*
3005—BRIDE FOR REAL *

*The Volakis Vow

CHAPTER ONE

VITALE ROCCANTI was a banker descended from a very old and aristocratic European family. Opening the private investigator's file on his desk, he studied the photograph of four people seated at a dining table. The Greek billionaire, Sergios Demonides, was entertaining Monty Blake, the British owner of the Royale hotel chain, his highly ornamental wife, Ingrid and their daughter, Zara.

Zara, nicknamed Tinkerbelle by the media for her celebrity status, her silver-gilt-coloured hair and fairy-like proportions, wore what appeared to be an engagement ring. Evidently the rumours of a buyout anchored by a family alliance were true. Most probably Demonides' loathing for publicity lay behind the lack of an official announcement but it certainly did look as though a marriage was on the cards.

Vitale, renowned for his shrewd brain and ruthless pursuit of profit, frowned. His lean, darkly handsome face hardened, his firm mouth compressing. His dark gaze flared gold with angry bitterness because it could only sicken him to see Monty Blake still smiling and at the top of his game. For a fleeting instant he allowed himself to recall the loving sister who had drowned when he was thirteen years old and his stomach clenched at the recollection of the savage loss that had left him alone in an inhospitable world. His sister had been the only person who had ever truly loved him. And the moment that he had worked towards for the better part of twenty years had finally arrived, for Blake looked to be on the brink of his greatest ever triumph. If Vitale waited any longer his prey might well become untouchable as the father-in-law of so powerful a man as Sergios Demonides. Yet how had Blake contrived to catch a fish as big as Demonides in his net? Apart from the little known fact that the Royale hotel chain had once belonged to Demonides' grandfather, what was the connection?

Were the oft-publicised charms of Tinkerbelle, whose brain was said to be as lightweight as her body, the only source of Blake's unexpected good fortune? Was she truly the sole attraction? Vitale had never let a woman come between him and his wits and would have assumed that Demonides had equal common sense. His mouth curled with derision. If he ensured that the engagement was broken the business deal might well go belly up as well and he would bring down Monty Blake, who desperately needed a buyer.

Vitale had never dreamt that he would have to get personal or indeed so unpleasantly close to his quarry to gain the revenge that his very soul craved for closure, but he remained convinced that Monty Blake's cruelty demanded an equal response. Should not the punishment be made to fit the crime? This was not the time to be fastidious, he reflected harshly. He could not afford to respect such boundaries. No, he only had one option: he would have to play dirty to punish the man who had abandoned his sister and her unborn child to their wretched fate.

A man who had always enjoyed enormous success with women, Vitale studied his prey, Tinkerbelle. His shapely mouth quirked. In his opinion she fell easily into the acceptable damage category. And wasn't suffering supposed to form character? Huge blue eyes wide in her heart shaped face, Blake's daughter was undeniably beautiful, but she also looked as shallow as a puddle and was anything but a blushing virgin with tender feelings. Undoubtedly she would regret the loss of so wealthy a catch as Demonides but Vitale imagined that, like her glossy mother, she had the hide of a rhinoceros and the heart of a stone and would bounce back very quickly from the disappointment. And if he left her a little wiser, that would surely only be to her advantage…

'I can't believe you've agreed to marry Sergios Demonides,' Bee confessed, her green eyes bright with concern as she studied the younger woman.

Although Bee was only marginally taller than her diminutive half sibling, and the two women had the same father, Bee was built on very different lines. Zara looked delicate enough to blow away in a strong breeze but Bee had inherited her Spanish mother's heavy fall of dark brown hair and olive-tinted skin and she had substantial curves. Bee was the child of Monty Blake's first marriage, which had ended in divorce, but she and Zara were close. Monty had a third daughter called Tawny, the result of an extra-marital affair. Neither girl knew their youngest sister very well because Tawny's mother was very bitter about the way their father had treated her.

'Why wouldn't I have?' Zara shrugged a narrow shoulder, striving for a show of composure. She was very fond of Bee and she didn't want the other woman worrying about her, so she opted for a deliberately careless response. 'I'm tired of being single and I like kids—'

'How can you be tired of being single? You're only twenty-two and it's not as if you're in love with Demonides!' Bee protested, scanning her sibling's flawless face in disbelief.

'Well…er—'

'You can't love him—you hardly *know* him, for goodness' sake!' Bee exclaimed, quick to take advantage of Zara's hesitation. Although she had met Sergios Demonides only once, her shrewd powers of observation, followed up by some careful Internet research on the Greek tycoon, had warned her that he was altogether too tough a proposition for her tenderhearted sister. Demonides had a very bad reputation with women and he was equally renowned for his cold and calculating nature.

Zara lifted her chin. 'It depends what you want out of marriage and all Sergios wants is someone to raise the children that have been left to his care—'

Bee frowned at that explanation. 'His cousin's three kids?'

Zara nodded. Several months earlier Sergios' cousin and his wife had been killed in a car crash and Sergios had become their children's legal guardian. Her future husband was a forceful, sardonic and distinctly intimidating shipping magnate, who travelled a great deal and worked very long hours. If she was honest, and there were very few people in Zara's life whom she dared to be honest with, she had been considerably less intimidated by Sergios once he had confessed that the only reason he wanted a wife was to acquire a mother for the three orphans in his home. That was a role that Zara felt she could comfortably cope with.

The children, ranging in age from a six-month-old baby to a three-year-old, were currently being raised almost entirely by his staff. Apparently the children had not settled well in his household. Sergios might be a very rich and powerful man but his concern for the children had impressed her. The product of a dysfunctional background himself, Sergios wanted to do what was best for those children but he just didn't know how and he was convinced that a woman would succeed where he had failed.

For her own part, Zara was desperately keen to do something that would finally make her parents proud of her. Her twin Tom's tragic death at the tender age of twenty had ripped a huge hole in her family. Zara had adored her brother. She had never resented the fact that Tom was their parents' favourite, indeed had often been grateful that Tom's academic successes had taken parental attention away from her wounding failures. Zara had left school halfway through her A-levels because she was struggling to cope, while Tom had been studying for a business degree at university and planning to join their father in the family hotel business when he crashed his sports car, dying instantly.

Sadly for all of them, her charismatic and successful brother had been everything her parents had ever wanted and needed in a child, and since his death grief had made her father's dangerous temper rage out of control more often. If in some way Zara was able to compensate her parents for Tom's loss and her survival she was eager to do it. After all she had spent her life striving for parental approval without ever winning it. When Tom had died she had wondered why fate chose him rather than her as a sacrifice. Tom had often urged her to make more of her life, insisting that she shouldn't allow their father's low opinion of her abilities to influence her so much. On the day of Tom's funeral she had promised herself that in honour of her brother's memory she would in the future make the most of every opportunity and work towards making her parents happy again. And it was a sad fact that Zara's entire education had been geared towards being the perfect wife for a wealthy man and that the only way she would ever really please her parents would be by marrying a rich high-achiever.

The children in Sergios' London home had touched her heart. Once she had been an unhappy child so she knew something of how they felt. Looking into those sad little faces, she had felt that finally she could make a big difference in someone else's life. Sergios might not personally need her, but those children genuinely *did* and she was convinced that she could make a success of her role as a mother. That was something she could do, something she could shine at and that meant a lot to Zara.

What was more, when she had agreed to marry Sergios, her father had looked at her with pride for the first time in her life. She would never forget that moment or the glow of warmth, acceptance and happiness she had felt. Her father had smiled at her and patted her shoulder in an unprecedented gesture of affection. 'Well done,' he had said, and she would not have exchanged that precious moment of praise for a million pounds. Zara was also convinced that marriage to Sergios would give her freedom, which she had never known. Freedom primarily from her father, whose temper she had learned to fear, but also freedom from the oppressive expectations of her perfectly groomed, socially ambitious mother, freedom from the boring repetition of days spent shopping and socialising with the right people in the right places, freedom from the egotistical men relentlessly targeting her as the next notch on their bed post…freedom—she hoped—that would ultimately allow her to be herself for the first time ever.

'And what happens when you *do* meet someone you can love?' Bee enquired ruefully in the lingering silence.

'That's not going to happen,' Zara declared with confidence. She had had her heart broken when she was eighteen, and, having experienced that disillusionment, had never warmed the slightest bit to any man since then.

Bee groaned out loud. 'You've got to be over that lowlife Julian Hurst by now.'

'Maybe I've just seen too many men behaving badly to believe in love and fidelity,' Zara fielded with a cynical gleam in her big blue eyes. 'If they're not after my father's money, they're after a one night stand.'

'Well, you've never been that,' Bee remarked wryly, well aware that, regardless of the media reports that constantly implied that Zara had enjoyed a wide range of lovers, her sibling appeared to be sublimely indifferent to most of the men that she met.

'But who would ever believe it? Sergios doesn't care either way. He doesn't need me in that department—' Zara would not have dreamt of sharing how welcome that lack of interest was to her. Her reluctance to trust a man enough to engage in sexual intimacy was too private a fact to share, even with the sister that she loved.

Bee froze, an expression of even greater dismay settling on her expressive face. 'My goodness, are you telling me that you've actually agreed to have one of those *open* marriages with him?'

'Bee, I couldn't care less what Sergios does as long as he's discreet and that's exactly what he wants—a wife who won't interfere with his life. He likes it as it is.'

Her sister looked more disapproving than ever. 'It won't work. You're far too emotional to get into a relationship like that at such a young age.'

Zara lifted her chin. 'We made a bargain, Bee. He's

agreed that the kids and I can live in London and that as long as I don't work full-time I can continue to run Edith's business.'

Taken aback by that information, Bee shook her head and looked even more critical. Zara's parents had simply laughed when Zara's aunt, Edith, died and left her niece her small but successful garden design business, Blooming Perfect. The Blakes had sneered at the idea of their severely dyslexic daughter running any kind of a business, not to mention one in a field that required specialist knowledge. Their father had stubbornly ignored the fact that in recent years Zara, who had long shared her aunt's love of well-groomed outdoor spaces, had successfully taken several courses in garden design. Huge arguments had broken out in the Blake household when Zara stood up to her controlling snobbish parents and not only refused to sell her inheritance but also insisted on taking a close interest in the day to day running of the business.

'I want…I *need* to lead my own life,' Zara confided with more than a hint of desperation.

'Of course, you do.' Full of sympathy when she recognised the tears glistening in Zara's eyes, Bee gripped the younger woman's hands in hers. 'But I don't think marrying Sergios is the way to go about that. You're only going to exchange one prison for another. He will have just as much of an agenda as your parents. Please think again about what you're doing,' Bee urged worriedly. 'I didn't like the man when I met him and I certainly wouldn't trust him.'

Driving away from the specially adapted house that

Bee shared with her disabled mother, Zara had a lot on her mind. Zara knew that it didn't make much sense to marry in the hope of getting a new life but she was convinced that, as a renowned entrepreneur in his own right, Sergios would be much more tolerant and understanding of her desire to run her own business than her parents could ever be. He would be even happier to have a wife with her own interests, who had no need to look to him for attention, and her parents would at last be proud of her, proud and pleased that their daughter was the wife of such an important man. Why couldn't Bee understand that the marriage was a win-win situation for all of them? In any case, Zara could no more imagine falling in love again than she could imagine walking down the street stark naked. A marriage of convenience was much more her style because love made fools of people, she thought painfully.

Her mother, for a start, was wed to a man who regularly played away with other women. Ingrid, a former Swedish model from an impoverished background, idolised her husband and the luxury lifestyle and social status he had given her by marrying her. No matter what Monty Blake did or how often he lost his violent temper, Ingrid forgave him or blamed herself for his shortcomings. And behind closed doors, her father's flaws were a good deal more frightening than anyone would ever have guessed, Zara thought, suppressing a shiver of recoil.

A moment later, Zara parked outside Blooming Perfect's small nursery. Rob, the manager her father had hired, was in the cluttered little office and he got up with a grin when she came in. 'I was just about to call you—we have a possible commission from abroad.'

'From where?' Zara questioned in surprise.

'Italy. The client has seen one of the gardens your aunt designed in Tuscany and apparently he was very impressed.'

Zara frowned. They had had several potential clients who backed off again the minute they realised that her aunt was no longer alive. 'What did he say when you told him she passed away?'

'I told him you do designs very much in the spirit of Edith's work, although with a more contemporary approach,' Rob explained. 'He was still keen enough to invite you out there on an all-expenses-paid trip to draw up a design. I gather he's a developer and he's renovated this house and now he wants the garden to match. By the sounds of it, it's a big bucks project and the chance you've been waiting for.'

Rob passed her the notebook on his desk to let her see the details he had taken. Zara hesitated before extending a reluctant hand to accept the notebook. For the sake of appearances she glanced down at the handwriting but she was quite unable to read it. As a dyslexic, reading was always a challenge for her but she had always found that actual handwriting as opposed to type was even harder for her to interpret. 'My goodness, what an opportunity,' she remarked dutifully.

'Sorry, I forgot,' Rob groaned, belatedly registering what was amiss, for she had had to tell him about her dyslexia to work with him. He dealt with what she could not. Retrieving the notebook, he gave her the details verbally instead.

While he spoke Zara remained stiff with discomfiture because she cringed from the mortifying moments when she could not hide her handicap and colleagues were forced to make allowances for her. It took her right back to the awful days when her father had repeatedly hammered her with the word 'stupid' as he raged about her poor school reports. In her mind normal people could read, write and spell without difficulty and she hated that she was different and hated even more having to admit the problem to others.

But Zara's embarrassment faded as enthusiasm at the prospect of a genuine creative challenge took its place. Apart from the designs she had worked on with Edith, her experience to date encompassed only small city gardens created on a restricted budget. A larger scheme was exactly what her portfolio lacked and, handled well, would give Blooming Perfect the gravitas it needed to forge a fresh path without relying so heavily on her late aunt's reputation. In addition if she made such a trip now it would ensure that Sergios and her family appreciated how seriously she took her new career. Perhaps then her family would stop referring to the design firm as her hobby.

'Phone him back and make the arrangements,' she instructed Rob. 'I'll fly out asap.'

Leaving Rob, Zara drove off to check the progress of the two current jobs on their books and found one in order and the other at a standstill because a nest of piping that nobody had warned them about had turned up in an inconvenient spot. Soothing the customer and organising a contractor to take care of the problem took time and it was after six before Zara got back to her self-contained flat in her parents' house. She would have preferred greater independence but she was reluctant to leave her mother alone with her father and very much aware that Monty Blake made more effort to control his temper while his daughter was within hearing.

Her indoor pet rabbit, Fluffy, gambolled round her feet in the hall, welcoming her home. Zara fed the little animal and stroked her soft furry head. Within ten minutes of her return, Ingrid Blake, a beautiful rake thin woman who looked a good deal younger than her forty-three years, joined her daughter in her apartment.

'Where the heck have you been all afternoon?' her mother demanded impatiently and at the sound of that shrill tone Fluffy bolted back into her hutch.

'I was at the nursery and I had some jobs to check—'

'The nursery? *Jobs?*' Ingrid grimaced as if Zara had said a rude word. 'When is this nonsense going to stop, Zara? The nursery can only ever be an interest. The real business of your life is the wedding you have to arrange—there's dress fittings, caterers and florists to see and that's only the beginning—'

'I thought we had a wedding organiser to take care of most of that for us,' Zara responded evenly. 'I've made myself available for every appointment—'

'Zara,' Ingrid began in a tone of exasperation, 'don't be more stupid than you can help. A bride should take a more active role in her own wedding.'

'Don't be more stupid than you can help' was a comment that could still cut deep, like a knife slicing through tender flesh, for Zara still looked back on her school years as a nightmare. Her lack of achievement during that period was, even now, a deep source of shame to her.

'This *is* more your wedding than mine,' Zara finally felt pushed into pointing out, for she couldn't have cared less about all the bridal fuss and frills.

Ingrid clamped a thin hand to a bony hip and swivelled to study her daughter with angry eyes. 'What's that supposed to mean?'

'Only that you care about that sort of thing and I don't. I'm not being rude but I've got more on my mind than whether I should have pearls or crystals on my veil and Sergios won't care either. Don't forget that this is his second marriage,' Zara reminded her mother gently, seeking a soothing note rather than piling logs on the fire of her mother's dissatisfaction.

In the midst of the dispute, Rob phoned Zara to ask how soon she could fly to Italy and he kept her on the line while he reserved her a flight in only two days' time. Too impatient to wait for Zara to give her her full attention again, Ingrid stalked out of the apartment in exasperation.

Left alone again, Zara heaved a sigh of relief. At least in Italy she would have a break from the wedding hysteria. Nothing mattered more to her mother than the appearance of things. Zara's failure to hog the gossip columns with a string of upper class boyfriends had offended Ingrid's pride for years and her mother had revelled in Tom's escapades in nightclubs with his posh pals. Ingrid, however, was determined that her daughter's wedding would be the biggest, splashiest and most talked about event of the season.

Sometimes Zara marvelled that she could have so little in common with her parents. Yet Zara and her father's sixty-year-old unmarried sister had got on like a house on fire. Edith and Zara had shared the same joy in the tranquil beauty of a lovely garden and the same unadorned and practical outlook on the rest of life. Her aunt's death, which had occurred within months of her brother's car crash, had devastated Zara. Edith had always seemed so fit that her sudden death from a heart attack had come as a terrible shock.

Zara dressed with care for her flight to Italy, teaming a khaki cotton skirt and jacket with a caramel coloured tee and low-heeled shoes. She anchored her mass of pale hair on top of her head with a judicious clip and used the minimum of make-up, apprehensive that her youth and looks would work against her with the client. After all, nobody knew better than a girl christened a dumb blonde at fourteen that first impressions could count for a lot. But, at the same time, as she stepped off her flight to Pisa she knew that her brother, Tom, would have been proud of her for sticking to her guns when it came to Blooming Perfect and making it clear how close the business was to her heart.

A driver met her at the airport and she was whisked off in the air-conditioned comfort of a glossy black four-wheel drive. The stupendous rural scenery of misty wooded hillsides and ancient medieval towns soothed nerves left ragged by a last-minute difference of opinion with her mother, who had objected bitterly once she realised that Zara was flying off to Italy for a long weekend.

'And how is your fiancé going to feel about that?' Ingrid had fired at her daughter.

'I have no idea. I haven't heard from him in a couple of weeks but I left a message on his phone to let him know that I would be away,' Zara had countered gently, for Sergios was not in the habit of maintaining regular contact with her and she perfectly understood that he saw their marriage to be staged three months hence as being more of a practical than personal connection.

'He's a very busy man,' Ingrid had instantly argued on her future son-in-law's behalf.

'Yes and he doesn't feel the need to keep constant tabs on me,' Zara pointed out quietly. 'And neither should you. I haven't been a teenager for a long time.'

Ingrid had pursed her lips. 'It's not like you're the brightest spark on the block and you know how dangerously impulsive you can be—'

Recalling that dig as she was driven through the Tuscan hills, Zara felt bitter. Only once in her life had she been dangerously impulsive and had paid in spades for that miscalculation. Even four years on, Zara still burned and felt sick at the memory of the humiliation that Julian Hurst had inflicted on her. She had grown up very fast after that betrayal, but even though she had never been so foolish again her parents continued to regularly remind her of her lowest moment.

The car turned off the road and her thoughts promptly turned to where she was headed, she sat up straighter to peer out of the windows. The lane became steep. If the house stood on a hill, as seemed likely, the garden would have wonderful views. Her first glimpse of the old stone building basking in the late afternoon sunshine made her eyes widen with pleasure. A traditional set of box-edged beds adorned the front of the villa, which was much bigger and more imposing than she had expected. Designing anything for an individual who owned such a beautiful property would be a major creative challenge and she was thrilled at the prospect.

As the driver lifted out her weekend bag the front door opened and a dark-haired woman in her thirties, elegantly dressed in a business suit, greeted her. 'Signorina Blake? Welcome to the Villa di Sole. I'm Catarina—I work for Signore Roccanti. He will be here shortly. How was your flight?'

Ushered into an airy hall floored in pale limestone, Zara smiled and set down her bag. It was obvious that the newly renovated house was empty and she began to wonder where she would be staying the night. The chatty woman showed her round the property. Well over a hundred and fifty years old, the villa had undergone elegant modernisation. In every way it was a stunning conversion. Rooms had been opened up and extended, opulent bathrooms added and smooth expanses of natural stone flooring, concealed storage and high-tech heating, lighting and sound systems added to achieve a level of luxury that impressed even Zara.

Catarina was a blank wall as far as questions concerning the extensive grounds were concerned. She had no idea what her employer might want done with the garden or what the budget might be.

'Signore Roccanti has discriminating taste,' she remarked as Zara admired the fabulous view of hills covered with vineyards and olive groves.

Fine taste and plenty of cash with which to indulge it, Zara was reflecting when she heard the dulled roar of a powerful car engine at the front of the property. Catarina hurried off with a muttered apology and moments later Zara heard heavy footsteps ringing across the tiled entrance hall.

She glanced up just as a man appeared in the doorway and her breath tripped in her throat. Sunshine flooded through the windows, gleaming over his black hair and dark curling lashes while highlighting the stunning lines of his classic bone structure and beautifully modelled mouth. He was smoking hot and that acknowledgement startled her—it was rare for Zara to have such a strong, immediate response to a man.

'A business appointment overran. I'm sorry I kept you waiting, *signorina*,' he murmured smoothly, his dark reflective gaze resting on her.

'Call me Zara, and you are…?' Zara was trying not to stare. She picked up the edge of strain in her voice and hoped it wasn't equally audible to him. She extended her hand.

'Vitale Roccanti. So, you are Edith's niece,' he remarked, studying her from below those outrageously long lashes, which would have looked girlie on any less masculine face, as he shook her hand and released it again, the light brush of those long brown fingers sending tingles of awareness quivering all over her body. 'Forgive me if I comment that you don't look much like her. As I recall she was rather a tall woman—'

Zara stilled in surprise. 'You actually met Edith?'

'I was living at the Palazzo Barigo with my uncle's family when your aunt was designing the garden,' Vitale explained, his gaze momentarily resting on her slender hand and noting the absence of an engagement ring. Had she taken it off?

As he made that connection with the woman who had taught her almost everything she knew Zara relaxed and a smile stole the tension from her delicate features. 'It is the most wonderful garden and in all the professional design books…'

When she smiled, Vitale conceded, she shot up the scale from exceptionally pretty to exquisitely beautiful. The photos hadn't lied but they hadn't told the whole truth either. In the light her pale hair glittered like highly polished silver, her velvety skin was flawless and those eyes, lavender blue below arched brows, were as unusual as they were gorgeous. He reminded himself that he liked his women tall, dark and curvaceous. She was tiny and slender as a ribbon, her delicate curves barely shaping her T-shirt and skirt, but she was also, from her dainty ankles to her impossibly small waist, an incredibly feminine woman. As for that mouth, unexpectedly full and rosy and ripe, any man would fantasise about a mouth that alluring. Vitale breathed in slow and deep, willing back the libidinous surge at his groin. He had not expected her to have quite so much appeal in the flesh.

'Have you been outside yet?' Vitale enquired.

'No, Catarina was showing me the house when you arrived—it's most impressive,' Zara remarked, her gaze following him as he pressed a switch and the wall of glass doors began to slide quietly back to allow access onto the terrace. He moved with the silent grace of a panther on the prowl, broad shoulders, narrow hips and long elegant legs defined by his beautifully tailored grey designer suit. She found it difficult to remove her attention from him. He was one of those men who had only to enter a room to command it. Even in a crowd he would have stood out a mile with his exceptional height, assurance and innate sophistication.

'The garden should complement the house with plenty of outside space for entertaining,' he told her.

'I see there's a pool,' she remarked, glancing at the feature that was at least fifty years old and marooned like an ugly centrepiece in the lank, overgrown grass.

'Site a replacement somewhere where it will not be the main attraction.'

Zara tried not to pull a face at the news that that landscaper's bête noire, the swimming pool, was to feature in the design. After all, every job had its pitfalls and there was plenty of space in which to provide a well-screened pool area. 'I have to ask you—is this going to be your home? Will a family be living here?'

'Aim at giving the garden universal appeal,' he advised, his face uninformative.

Zara felt slightly foolish. Of course if the villa was to

be sold which was the most likely objective for a property developer, he would have no idea who the eventual owner would be. As she began to walk down the worn steps her heel skittered off the edge of one and his hands cupped her elbow to steady her. The faint scent of a citrus-based cologne flared her nostrils in the hot still air. When she reached level ground again he removed his hand without fanfare but she remained extraordinarily aware of his proximity, the height and strength of his long, lean frame, not to mention the unmistakeable aura of raw masculinity.

She needed measurements for the garden, all sorts of details, but Vitale Roccanti did not look like the patient type, happy to stand around and wait while she took notes. She would have to contain her eagerness to start work until her next visit. The garden ran right up to the edges of woodland and merged with the dark shade cast by the trees. But the open view to the south was nothing short of breathtaking.

Vitale watched her face light up as she caught the view of the hills with the sun starting to go down, bathing the trees in a golden russet light. Her habitually wary expression was transformed into one of open enjoyment. She was not at all what he had expected, being neither flirtatious nor giggly nor even high maintenance if that plain outfit was the norm for her. No make-up that he could see either, which was an even more unusual sight for a man accustomed to decorative women, who preferred to present a highly polished image for his benefit.

As Zara turned back to him her unusual lavender

eyes were shining at the prospect of the challenge before her. In such beautiful surroundings this was truly her dream job. 'How much land does this place have?'

The purity of her heart-shaped face, lit up with the unhidden enthusiasm of a child's, made the man watching her stare. *Per amor di Dio,* Vitale reflected involuntarily, what a piece of perfection she was! The unfamiliar thought jolted him and his hard bone structure tautened and shadowed.

'The land as far as you can see belongs to the house. It was once a substantial agricultural estate,' he explained. 'You'll be able to come back here to explore tomorrow. A vehicle will be placed at your disposal.'

Zara encountered stunning dark golden eyes with the shrewd watchful penetration of gold-tipped arrows. Dark-hued, deep-set, very sexy eyes surrounded by inky black lashes and blessed with extraordinary impact. Goose bumps erupted on Zara's arms. Her mouth ran dry, her tummy executing a sudden somersault that made her tense and dizzy. 'Thanks, that will be very helpful,' she responded, striving to overcome the way she was feeling by making herself remember Julian and the pain and humiliation that he had inflicted on her.

'Prego!' Vitale answered lightly, showing her back indoors and escorting her back through the silent house.

In the hall she bent down to lift her weekend bag.

'I have it,' Vitale said, reaching the bag a split second in advance of her.

She followed him outside and hovered while he paused to lock up. He opened the door of the black

Lamborghini outside, stowed her bag and stepped back for her to get in.

'Where will I be staying?' she asked as she climbed into the passenger seat, nervous fingers smoothing down her skirt as it rose a little too high above her knees.

'With me. I have a farmhouse just down the hill. It will be a convenient base for you.' His attention inescapably on those dainty knees and pale slim thighs, Vitale was thinking solely of parting them and he caught himself on that X-rated image with a frown.

What the hell was the matter with him? Anyone could have been forgiven for thinking that he was sex-starved, which couldn't be further from the truth. Vitale scheduled sex into his itinerary as efficiently as business appointments. He had lovers in more than one European city, discreet, sophisticated women who knew better than to expect a lasting commitment from him. There were no emotional scenes or misunderstandings in Vitale's well-ordered life and that was how he liked it. He had not rebuilt his life from the ground up by allowing weakness to exist in his character. He had no expectations of people and he certainly didn't trust them. If there were no expectations there was less chance of disappointment. He had learned not to care about women, especially not to love them. Life had taught him that those you cared about moved on, died or betrayed you. In the aftermath of such experiences being alone hurt even more but it was safer not to feel anything for anyone. That credo had served him well, taking him from extreme poverty and deprivation to the comfortable cultured life of a multimillionaire, who seemed to make more money with every passing year.

CHAPTER TWO

THE farmhouse sat a good distance from the mountain road, accessed by a track that stretched almost a kilometre into dense woods. Built of soft ochre-coloured stone and roofed in terracotta, the property was surrounded by a grove of olive trees with silvery foliage that seemed to shimmer in the fading light.

'Very picturesque,' Zara pronounced breathlessly, belatedly registering that she had allowed herself to be brought to an isolated place in the countryside by a man whom she knew almost nothing about! She mentally chastised herself for her lack of caution.

As her lips parted to suggest that she would prefer a hotel—at her own expense—a plump little woman in an apron appeared at the front door and smiled widely.

'My housekeeper, Guiseppina, has come out to welcome you. Be warned, she will try to fatten you up,' Vitale remarked teasingly as he swung out of the car.

The appearance of another woman relieved much of Zara's concern, although a stubborn thought at the back of her mind was already leafing through various murders in which the killers had enjoyed female companionship and support in which to commit their crimes. Her colourful imagination had often been considered one of her biggest flaws by her teachers. 'I think I would prefer to be in a hotel—I'll settle my own bills,' she muttered tautly.

In considerable surprise, for he was accustomed to women seizing on every opportunity to enjoy his full attention, Vitale recognised her apprehension and murmured, 'If you would be more comfortable staying in this house alone I will use my city apartment while you are here. It is not a problem.'

Flushing in embarrassment, afraid that she might have sounded a little hysterical while also being soothed by his offer, Zara hastened to recant. 'No, that's really not necessary. I think it's the fact I know virtually nothing about you except that you're a property developer—'

'But I'm not…a property developer,' Vitale confided in a ludicrous tone of apology.

Zara studied his lean bronzed features with a bemused frown. 'You're…*not*?' A helpless laugh bubbled out of her throat because there was something very amusing about the way in which he had broken that news.

'I'm a banker,' Vitale admitted.

'Oh…' Zara exclaimed, nonplussed by that level admission, there being nothing flashy, threatening or indeed exciting about bankers in her past experience.

'The property developing is only a pastime.' Her patent lack of interest in his admission set his teeth on edge a little. Had he been spoilt by all the women who hung on his every word and eagerly tried to find out everything about him?

Bubbling Italian like a fountain, Giuseppina was a bustling whirlwind of a woman and she instantly took centre stage. Although Zara didn't understand much of what she was saying, it didn't inhibit Giuseppina's chatter. She drew Zara eagerly into the house and straight up the creaking oak staircase to a charming bedroom with painted furniture and crisp white bed linen. Zara glanced with satisfaction at the en suite bathroom. The walls might be rustic brick and the furniture quirky and antique but, like the Villa di Sole, every contemporary comfort had been incorporated.

A light knock sounded on the ajar door. Vitale set her bag down on the wide-planked floor. 'Dinner will be served in an hour and a half. I hope you're hungry. I bring guests here so rarely that Giuseppina seems determined to treat us to a banquet.'

Zara glanced at him and for an instant, as she collided with dark eyes that glowed like the warmest, deepest amber in the fading light, it was as though her every defence fell down and she stood naked and vulnerable. For a terrifying energising moment she was electrified by the breathtaking symmetry and beauty of his face regardless of the five o'clock shadow of stubble steadily darkening his jaw line. She wondered what it would feel like to kiss him and the passage of blood through her veins seemed to slow and thicken while her heart banged behind her ribs and her breath dragged through her tight throat.

As Giuseppina took her leave, her sturdy shoes ringing out her descent of the stairs, Vitale held Zara's gaze, his eyes scorching gold, lashes dipping low as though to conceal them. 'I'll see you at dinner,' he told her huskily, backing away.

As the door shut on his departure Zara was trembling. She felt too warm. Unfreezing, she darted into the bathroom to splash her face with cold water. Her hands shook as she snatched up the towel to dry herself again. Never before had she felt so aware of a man. The feelings that had drawn her to Julian as a teenager paled utterly in comparison. She stripped where she stood to go for a shower. What was happening to her? She had decided a long time ago that she just wasn't that sexual a being. Only once had a man made Zara want to surrender her virginity and that man had been Julian, but if she was truthful she had only been willing to sleep with him because she had assumed that it was expected. When in fact Julian had put greed ahead of lust in his priorities, Zara had been left a virgin and a very much sadder and wiser one. So what was different about Vitale Roccanti?

After all, in August she was supposed to be marrying Sergios Demonides and, having thoroughly weighed up the pros and cons, she had reached that decision on her own. All right, she didn't love the man she had promised to marry and he didn't love her, but she did respect the commitment she had made to him. Loyalty and respect *mattered* to her. Was it stress that was making her feel edgy and out of sync? Or was Bee's warning that she might fall for another man after she married working on some level of her brain to make her more than usually aware of an attractive man? Vitale *was* an extraordinarily handsome man and very charismatic. That was fact. Possibly she was more nervous about getting married than she had been prepared to admit even to herself. And for all she knew Vitale Roccanti was a married man. Yanking a towel off the rail as she stepped out of the shower, she grimaced at that suspicion. At the very least he might be involved in a steady relationship. And why on earth should that matter to her? Not only did it not matter to her whether he was involved or otherwise with a woman, it was none of her business, she told herself staunchly. In the same way it was none of Vitale's business that she was committed to Sergios. She thought it was unfortunate, though, that Sergios had chosen not to give her an engagement ring. But there was still no good reason why she should bother telling Vitale that she was getting married in three months' time. Why was she getting so worked up?

Releasing her hair from the clip, she let the silvery strands fall loose round her shoulders and she put on the print tea dress she had packed for more formal wear. Dinner was served on the terrace at the rear of the property. A candle flickered on the beautifully set table in the shade of a venerable oak tree. Her slim shoulders unusually tense, Zara left the shelter of the house.

A glass of wine in one hand, Vitale was talking on a cell phone in a liquid stream of Italian. He was casually seated on the edge of a low retaining wall, a pair of chinos and an open shirt having replaced the suit he had worn earlier. Black hair still spiky from a shower, he had shaved, baring the sleek planes of his features and throwing into prominence his beautifully shaped mouth. Her heart seemed to take a flying leap inside her body, making it incredibly difficult to catch her breath.

'Zara,' he murmured softly in greeting, switching off the phone and tossing it aside.

'I used to hate my name but suppose everyone does at some stage when they're growing up,' Zara confided, aware that she was chattering too much in an effort to hide her self-consciousness but quite unable to silence herself.

'It's a pretty name.'

Madly aware of his intense scrutiny, Zara felt her cheeks warm. For goodness' sake, relax, she urged herself, exasperated by her oversensitive reaction to him. He sprang fluidly upright, his every physical move laced with easy strength and grace, and asked her if she would like some wine. He returned from the house bearing a glass.

It was a warm evening. She settled into the seat he pulled out from the table for her and Giuseppina appeared with the first course, a mouth-watering selection of *antipasti*. Her bright dark eyes danced between them with unconcealed curiosity and romantic hopes.

'I'm twenty-nine. She thinks I ought to be married by now with a family and she keeps on warning me that all the best girls have already been snapped up,' Vitale told her in an undertone, his eyes alive with vibrant amusement.

Surprised by his candour, Zara laughed. 'Have they been?'

'I don't know. The women with wedding rings in their eyes are the ones I've always avoided,' Vitale volunteered.

Zara reckoned that if she was truly the honest person she had always believed she was she would be telling him that she was within a few months of getting married herself. Yet while the admission was on her tongue she could not quite bring herself to speak up. At the same time she could not help wondering if Vitale could actually be warning her off. Was it possible that he was letting her know that he had only ever been in the market for a casual affair?

Whatever, there was no future or sense in succumbing to any kind of entanglement with him and she was far too sensible to make such a mistake. In honour of that conviction and impervious to his polite look of surprise, Zara dug her notebook out of her bag and began to quiz him about his garden preferences and his budget. The main course of steak was so tender it melted on her tongue and it was served with a tomato salad and potato and cheese croquettes. She ate with unbridled pleasure for it was, without a doubt, an exceptional meal, and when she could bring herself to set down her knife and fork she took notes.

'This is not quite how I envisaged dining with you,' Vitale remarked wryly. It hadn't escaped his notice that she ignored any hint of flirtation, preferring to maintain a professional barrier he had not expected. Of course she was clever enough to know that lack of interest only made the average man keener, he decided, unwilling to concede the possibility that she might be genuinely indifferent to him.

Although he was taken aback by her eagerness to work he was pleasantly surprised by her healthy appetite and the way in which she savoured Giuseppina's renowned cuisine, for he was accustomed to women who agonised over eating anything more calorific than a lettuce leaf. 'You should be relaxing. You can work tomorrow.'

'But I'm only here for a couple of days. I need to make the most of my time,' Zara told him lightly as Guiseppina set a lemon tart on the table and proceeded to cut slices. 'And if I do find myself with a spare couple of hours I'm hoping to try and visit the garden my aunt Edith made at the Palazzo Barigo.'

'Have you not already seen it?'

'I've never been to this area before. My parents don't do rural holidays.' Her sultry mouth quirked at the mere idea of her decorative mother in a countryside setting. 'I did ask my aunt once if she would like to come back and see the garden and she said no, that gardens change with the passage of time and that she preferred to remember it as it was when it was new.'

'If I can arrange it before you leave I will take you to the Palazzo Barigo for a tour,' Vitale drawled softly, lifting the bottle to top up her wine glass.

'No more for me, thanks,' Zara told him hurriedly. 'I get giggly too easily, so I never drink much.'

Vitale was sardonically amused by that little speech. She was putting up barriers as prickly as cactus leaves and visibly on her guard. But he was too experienced not to have noticed her lingering appraisals and he was convinced that she wanted him even though she was trying to hide the fact. Erotic promise thrummed through his body, setting up a level of anticipation beyond anything he had ever experienced.

Vitale was as well travelled as Zara and they shared amusing anecdotes about trips abroad, discovering that their sense of humour was amazingly similar. He moved his hands expressively while he talked and slowly but surely she found herself watching him like a hawk. When all of a sudden she collided with his scorching golden eyes, she couldn't even manage to swallow. The truth that she couldn't stifle her physical response to him alarmed her. She was not in full control of her response to Vitale Roccanti and disturbingly that took her back to her ordeal with Julian. She breathed in slow and deep and steady, mentally fighting to step back from her reactions. Vitale was gorgeous but not for her. She didn't want to dip a toe in the water, she didn't want to get her fingers burnt either. Even if it killed her she was determined to retain her self-respect.

'I hope you won't think I'm being rude but I've had a lot of late nights this week and I would like to turn in now so that I can make an early start in the morning,' Zara proffered with a bright smile of apology.

Vitale accepted her decision with good grace, rising immediately to his feet. Her cheeks warmed at the sudden suspicion that he might only have been entertaining her out of courtesy. Not every guy wanted to jump her bones, she reminded herself irritably.

At the foot of the stairs, she hovered, disconcertingly reluctant to leave him even though she had carefully engineered her own exit. 'Will I see you in the morning?' she asked breathlessly.

'I doubt it. I'll be leaving soon after six,' Vitale imparted, watching her slim figure shift restively. His level of awareness was at such a pitch it was not only his muscles that ached.

Still unable to tear herself away, Zara looked up at him, focusing on the irresistible dark glitter of his stunning eyes and his perfect lips. He was downright drenched in sex appeal and she wanted to touch him so badly her fingertips tingled. The hunger he was suddenly making no attempt to hide made her feel all hot and shivery deep down inside.

'But before we part, *cara mia…*' Vitale purred, pure-bred predator on the hunt as he closed long, deft fingers round her arm to ease her closer.

He took Zara by surprise and she froze in dismay, nostrils flaring on the scent of his cologne. 'No,' she said abruptly, planting both her palms firmly to his broad chest to literally push him back from her. 'I don't know what you think I'm doing here but I'm certainly not here for this.'

Ditching the smile ready to play about his beautifully sculpted mouth, Vitale lifted a sardonic brow. 'No?'

'You have a hell of an opinion of yourself, don't you?' The tart rejoinder just leapt off Zara's tongue, fierce annoyance rattling through her at his arrogant attitude. Evidently he had expected her to succumb rather than shoot him down and the knowledge infuriated her, for she had met too many men who expected her to be a pushover.

His dark, heavily lashed eyes flashed with anger and then screened. 'Perhaps I misread the situation—'

'Yes, you definitely did,' Zara retorted defensively. 'I'm grateful for your hospitality and I've enjoyed your company but that's as far as it goes! Goodnight, Vitale.'

But as she hastened up the stairs and hurriedly shut her bedroom door she felt like a total fraud. Exit shocked virginal heroine stage left, she mocked inwardly, her face burning. He had not misread the situation as much as she would have liked to believe. She *did* find him incredibly attractive and clearly he had recognised the fact and tried to act on it. She was not the undersexed woman she had come to believe she was. But what a time to make such a discovery about herself! Why now? Why now when she was committed to marrying another man? Even though her bridegroom had no desire to share a bed with her, her susceptibility to Vitale Roccanti's lethal dark charisma made her feel guilty and disloyal.

She lay in bed studying the crescent of the moon gleaming through the curtains. Vitale was simply a temptation she had to withstand and maybe it was good that she should be reminded now that being a married woman would demand circumspection from her. In the future she would be more on her guard. But she could not forget that even in a temper she had still not told him that she was getting married that summer.

CHAPTER THREE

AT WAR with herself, Zara tossed and turned for a good part of the night, wakening to a warm room bathed in the bright light filtering through the thin curtains. Seating her on the terrace, Giuseppina brought her a breakfast of fresh peaches, milky coffee and bread still warm from the oven served with honey. Birds were singing in the trees, bees buzzing and golden sunshine drenched the country valley below the house. It was a morning to be glad to be alive, not to brood on what could not be helped. So, a handsome Italian had made a mild pass at her, why was she agonising over the fact? The attraction had been mutual? So, she was human, fallible.

Giuseppina brought her keys to the car and the villa and Zara left the house to climb into the sturdy pickup truck parked outside. In the early morning quiet the garden of the villa was a wonderful haven of peace. Grateful that it was still relatively cool, Zara took measurements and sat down on a wrought iron chair in the shade of the house to do some preliminary sketches. She chose the most suitable site for the pool first and, that achieved, her ideas were free to flow thick and fast. For the front of the house she wanted a much more simple and soft approach than the current formal geometry of the box-edged beds. So engrossed was she that she didn't hear the car pulling up at the front and she glanced up in surprise when she heard a door slam inside the house.

Vitale strolled outside, a vision of sleek dark masculinity sheathed in summer casuals, a sweater knotted round his shoulders with unmistakeable Italian style. She scrambled up, her heart going bang-bang-bang inside her chest and her mouth dry as a bone.

'Time for lunch,' he told her lazily.

Zara glanced at her watch for the first time since she had arrived and was startled to find that the afternoon was already well advanced. It had taken his reminder for her to notice that her tummy was hollow with hunger. 'I lost track of time…'

Vitale moved closer to glance curiously at the sheaf of sketches she was gathering up. 'Anything for me to see yet?'

'I prefer to submit a design only when I'm finished,' she told him evenly, accustomed to dealing with impatient clients. 'I've been working on some options for the hard landscaping first.'

He studied her from beneath the dark lush screen of his lashes. Even without a speck of make-up and clad in sexless shorts and a loose shirt, she was a true beauty. Tendrils of wavy silvery hair had worked loose from the clasp she wore to cluster round her damp temples and fall against her cheekbones. Her lavender eyes were wide above heat-flushed cheeks, her temptress mouth lush and natural pink. The tightening heaviness at his groin made his teeth clench. She looked very young, very fresh and impossibly sexy. He remembered the rumour that Monty Blake had paid a fortune to suppress pornographic pictures taken by some boyfriend of hers when she was only a teenager and he reminded himself that it was quite some time since Zara Blake was in a position to claim that level of innocence.

Disturbingly conscious of his measuring appraisal, Zara packed away her sketch pad and pencils. The coarse cotton of her shirt was rubbing against her swelling nipples. As was often her way in a hot climate she had not worn a bra and in his presence her body was determined to misbehave and she was insanely aware of those tormented tips.

'I'm taking you to the Palazzo Barigo,' Vitale volunteered, walking her back through the house and out to the Lamborghini.

Edith's garden, he was taking her to see Edith's garden! Zara almost whooped with delight and a huge grin curved her soft lips; she turned shining eyes on him. 'That's wonderful—is it open to the public, then?'

'Not as a rule.'

'Of course, you said it belonged to your uncle,' she recalled, reckoning that, had she been on her own, she might not have been granted access. 'Thank you so much for making this possible. I really appreciate it. Should I get changed or will I do as I am? I haven't got many clothes with me. I like to travel light.'

'There is only staff at the palazzo at present. You can be as casual as you like,' Vitale responded lightly.

'What will we do about the car I drove here?' she asked belatedly.

'It will be picked up later.'

The Palazzo Barigo lay over an hour's drive away. Zara used a good part of the journey to sound him out on different kinds of stone and then she discussed the need for a lighting consultant. She found him more silent and less approachable than he had seemed the night before. Had her rejection caused offence? It was probably her imagination, she thought ruefully, but once or twice she thought he seemed distinctly tense. His lean, hard-boned face was taut in profile, his handsome mouth compressed.

'How did you spend your morning?' she enquired when she had failed to draw him out on other topics.

'At the office.'

'Do you often work at weekends?'

'I was in New York last week. Work piled up while I was away.' His fingers flexed and tightened again round the leather steering wheel.

'This landscape is beautiful. No wonder Edith felt inspired working here.'

'You talk a lot, don't you?' Vitale sighed. The views she was admiring were painfully familiar to his grim gaze. He felt as though his world were turning full circle, bringing him back to the place where the events that had indelibly changed his life had begun. Yet conversely he was conscious that only two years earlier he had taken a step that ensured he could never hope to escape that past.

Zara could feel her face reddening. She did talk quite a bit and it wasn't exactly intellectual stuff. Perhaps he found her boring. Annoyance leapt through her as she fiercely suppressed a sense of hurt. He wasn't her boyfriend, he wasn't her lover, he wasn't anything to her and his opinion should not matter to her in the slightest.

'I'm sorry, that was rude,' Vitale drawled softly, shooting the powerful car off the road and below a worn stone archway ornamented with a centrally placed Grecian urn. 'I'm afraid I've had a rough morning but that is not an excuse for ill humour. I find spending time with you very relaxing.'

Zara wasn't quite convinced by that turnaround and when he parked she got out and said stiffly, 'You know, if there's only staff here, you could leave me to explore on my own for an hour. You don't need to stay—'

'I want to be with you, *angelina mia*,' Vitale intoned across the bonnet, whipping off his sunglasses to view her with level dark golden eyes. 'Why do you think I arranged this outing? Only to please you.'

As Zara could think of no good reason why he should have bothered otherwise, the anxious tension fell from her heart-shaped face. 'I'm no good with moody guys,' she confided with a wry look. 'They make me uncomfortable.'

'I'm not moody.'

Aware of the powerful personality that drove him, Zara didn't quite believe him on that score. He might not be subject to moods as a rule but he was definitely a very driven and strong individual. She was convinced that he could be stubborn and tough and a bit of a maverick but she had no idea how she could be so sure of those traits when she had only met him the day before. And yet she *was* sure. In much the same way she read the strain in his dark golden gaze and realised for the first time that he wasn't just flirting with her, he wasn't just playing a sexual game like so many of the men she had met. Vitale Roccanti was keen to soothe the feelings he had hurt. He sincerely cared about her opinion. Heartened by that conviction, she tried not to smile.

Vitale lifted out the picnic basket Giuseppina had made up and tossed Zara a cotton rug to carry and extended his free hand to her. 'Let's find somewhere to eat…'

'The orchard,' she suggested dreamily, already mentally visualising the garden design she had often studied.

In the heat of the afternoon they strolled along gravelled paths. The clarity of her aunt's talent as a designer was still as clear as it must have been forty years earlier when it was first created. 'The garden's been replanted,' Zara registered in surprise and pleasure, for she had expected to see overgrown shrubs and trees, the once noticeable lines of her aunt's vision blurred by many years of growth.

'Eighteen months ago.' Vitale's explanation was crisp, a little distracted. As she stood there against the backdrop of a great yew tree he was remembering his sister dancing along the same path in a scarlet silk gown for a fashion photographer's benefit, her lovely face stamped with the detached hauteur of a model, only the sparkle of her eyes revealing her true joyous mood. 'For a while the house and garden were open as a tourist attraction.'

'But not now,' Zara gathered.

'The owner cherishes his privacy.'

'It's almost selfish to own something this beautiful and refuse to share it with other people,' Zara contended in a tone of censure, lavender eyes darting in every direction because there was so much for her to take in.

His handsome mouth quirked as he watched her clamber unselfconsciously onto a stone bench in an effort to gain a better overall view above the tall evergreen hedges. 'The temple on the hill above the lake offers the best prospect.'

Zara's fine brows connected in a sudden frown. 'There was no temple in the original scheme.'

'Perhaps the owner felt he could add a little something without destroying the symmetry of the whole,' Vitale murmured a tinge drily.

Zara went pink. 'Of course. I think it's wonderful that he thought enough of the garden to maintain it and secure its future for another generation.'

Vitale shot her a searching glance, much amused against his will by her quick recovery. She was a lousy liar, having something of a child's artlessness in the way that she spoke and acted without forethought. She had no patience either. He watched her hurry ahead of him with quick light steps, a tiny trim figure with silvery pale hair catching and holding the sunlight. When he had seen the photos of her he had assumed the hair was dyed but it looked strikingly natural, perfectly attuned to her pale Nordic skin and unusual eyes. He would have to get her clothes off to explore the question further and that was a prospect that Vitale was startled to discover that he could hardly wait to bring about.

Monty Blake's daughter had an unanticipated charm all of her own. Even in the casual clothes her quintessential femininity, dainty curves and deeply disconcerting air of spontaneity turned him on hard and fast. It was years since any woman had had that effect on him and he didn't like it at all. Vitale much preferred a predictable low level and controllable response to a woman. He did not like surprises.

Beyond an avenue of cypresses and the vista of a picturesque town clinging to the upper slopes of a distant hill, the garden became less formal and a charming winding path led them to the cherry orchard. Wild flowers laced the lush grass and Zara hovered rather than spread the rug because it seemed almost a desecration to flatten those blooms. Vitale had no such inhibitions, however and he took the rug from her and cast it down. He was wondering if she could possibly have chosen the private location in expectation and encouragement of a bout of alfresco sex. No way, absolutely no way, Vitale decided grittily, was he sinking his famously cool reputation to fool about in long grass like a testosterone-driven teenager.

Seated unceremoniously on her knees and looking not remotely seductive, however, Zara was already digging through the basket and producing all sorts of goodies. 'I'm really hungry,' she admitted.

Vitale studied her and decided that he was becoming too set in his ways. Maybe he could bite the bullet if the only option was making out in the grass. He poured chilled white wine while she set out plates and extracted thin slices of prosciutto ham, wedges of onion and spinach frittata, a mozzarella and tomato salad and a bowl of pasta sprinkled with zucchini blossoms. It was a colourful and enticing spread.

'Giuseppina is a treasure,' Zara commented, digging in without further ado to a wedge of frittata washed down with wine from a moisture-beaded glass.

'I'm an excellent cook,' Vitale volunteered unexpectedly. 'Giuseppina is a recent addition to my household.'

'I can just about make toast,' Zara told him cheerfully. 'My older sister, Bee, is always offering to teach me to cook but I'm more into the garden than the kitchen.'

'I didn't know you had a sister.'

Zara kicked off her shoes and lounged back on one elbow to munch through ham and a generous spoonful of the juicy tomato salad with unconcealed enjoyment. 'Dad has three daughters from two marriages and one affair. He's a bit of a womaniser,' she muttered, downplaying the truth to an acceptable level.

'Is he still married to your mother?'

Worrying at her full lower lip, Zara compressed her sultry mouth. 'Yes, but he's had other interests along the way—she turns a blind eye. Gosh, I don't know why I'm telling you that. It's private.'

'Obviously it bothers you,' Vitale remarked perceptively.

It had always bothered Zara. Several years earlier, Edith had gently warned her niece to mind her own business when it came to her parents' marriage, pointing out that some adults accepted certain compromises in their efforts to maintain a stable relationship. 'I think fidelity is very important…'

Thinking of the wedding plans that he already knew were afoot in London on her behalf, Vitale almost laughed out loud in derision at that seemingly naïve declaration. He supposed it sounded good and that many men, burned by female betrayal, would be impressed by such a statement. More cynical and never ever trusting when it came to her sex, Vitale veiled his hard dark eyes lest he betray his scorn.

Zara could feel hot colour creeping across her face. She believed fidelity was important yet she had agreed to marry a man who had no intention of being faithful to her. Suddenly and for the first time she wondered if Bee had been right and if she could be making the biggest mistake of her life. But then, she reminded herself quickly, she would not be entering a real marriage with Sergios. In a perfect world and when people loved each other fidelity was important, she rephrased for her own benefit. Feeling panicky and torn in opposing directions by the commitment she had so recently entered, Zara drained her wine glass and let Vitale top it up.

'How do you feel about it?' Zara pressed her silent companion nonetheless because she really wanted to know his answer.

'As though we've strayed into a dialogue that is far too serious for such a beautiful day.'

Was that an evasion? Vitale was very adroit with words and Zara, who more often than not said the wrong thing to the wrong person at the wrong time, was reluctantly impressed by his sidestepping of what could be a controversial subject. More than anything else, though, she respected honesty, but she knew that some regarded her love of candour as a sign of immaturity and social awkwardness.

'I could never, ever forgive lies or infidelity,' Zara told him.

Watching sunshine make her hair flare like highly polished silver, her eyes mysterious lavender pools above her pink pouting mouth as she sipped her wine, Vitale reflected that had he been the susceptible type he might have been in danger around Zara Blake. After all she was a beauty, surprisingly individual and very appealing in all sorts of unexpected ways. That radiant smile, for instance, offered a rare amount of joie de vivre. But most fortunately for him, Vitale reminded himself with satisfaction, he was cooler than ice in the emotion department and all too aware of whose blood ran in her veins.

Barely a minute later and without even thinking about what he was going to do, Vitale leant down and pressed his sensual mouth to Zara's. He tasted headily of wine. His lips were warm and hard and the clean male scent of him unbelievably enticing. Zara stretched closer, increasing the pressure of his mouth on hers with a needy little sound breaking low in her throat.

Her hands curved to his strong, muscular shoulders and, as though she had given him a green light to accelerate the pace, the kiss took off like a rocket. His hot tongue pierced between her lips and she shivered violently, erotic signals racing through her slight length. A flood of heat travelled from the pinched taut tips of her breasts to the liquid tension pooling at the heart of her. Her heart thumping out a tempestuous beat, she dug her fingers into his silky black hair and kissed him back with a hunger she couldn't repress.

Within seconds she was on her back, Vitale lying half over her with one lean thigh settling between hers. On one level she tensed, ready to object the way she usually would have done if a man got too close, but on another unfamiliar level his weight, proximity and the fiery hunger of his kiss somehow combined in a soaring crescendo of sensuality to unleash a powerful craving she had never felt before.

'You taste so good,' Vitale growled huskily, '*so* unbelievably good, *angelina mia*.'

He was talking too much and she didn't want him talking, she wanted him kissing, and she pulled him back down to her with impatient hands. He reacted to that shameless invitation with a driving passion that thrilled her. His mouth ravished hers, his tongue darting and sliding in the tender interior and the thunderous wave of desire screaming through her was almost unbearable. Long fingers slid below her top, travelling over her narrow ribcage to close round a small rounded breast. He found the beaded tip, squeezed it and she arched off the ground, shattered by the arrow of hot liquid need shooting down into her pelvis. And that jolt of soul stealing desire was sufficient to spring her out of the sensual spell he had cast.

Eyes bright with dismay, Zara had only a split second to focus over his shoulder on the trees around her and recall where she was and what she was doing. Shot back to awareness with a vengeance, she gasped, 'No!' as she pushed at his shoulders and rolled away from him the instant he drew back.

Still on another plane, Vitale blinked, dazed at what had just happened. *Almost* happened, he corrected mentally. *Dio mio,* they were lying in an orchard and there wasn't even the remotest chance that he would have let matters proceed any further. She was like a stick of dynamite, he thought next, dark colour scoring his high cheekbones as he struggled to catch his breath and withstand the literal pain of his fully aroused body. A woman capable of making him behave like that in a public place ought to carry a government health warning. Overconfident, he had underestimated the extent of her pulling power, a mistake he would not repeat, he swore vehemently.

'I'm sorry…' Zara's teeth almost chattered in the aftershock of having called a crushing halt to that runaway passion. 'But someone might have come along,' she completed lamely, wondering if she seemed dreadfully old-fashioned and a bit hysterical to a guy of his experience. After all he had only kissed her and touched her breast and she had thrown him off as if he had assaulted her.

'No, I'm sorry,' Vitale fielded, reaching for her hand,

the nails of which were digging into the surface of the rug in a revealing show of discomfiture, and straightening her fingers in a calming gesture. 'I didn't think.'

It was an admission that very nearly choked Vitale Roccanti, who, with the patience and power of a Machiavelli, had planned and plotted his every move from the age of thirteen and never once failed to deliver on any count. Zara, however, was soothed by his apology and his grip on her hand. In her experience not all men were so generous in the aftermath of thwarted desire.

In seemingly silent mutual agreement they put away the picnic and folded the rug to start back to the car. She had barely seen the garden but it no longer had the power to dominate her thoughts. Her entire focus was now centred on Vitale. Was this what an infatuation felt like? Or was it something more? Was he a man she could fall in love with? How did she know? Was she crazy to wonder such a thing? Julian had been her first love but he had never had the power to make her feel the way Vitale did. Sadly she had been too young at eighteen to understand that there should be more said and more felt in a relationship with a future.

Just before she climbed back into the car, a gardener working at a border across the front lawn raised a hand to acknowledge Vitale. Of course, his uncle's employees would know him. She watched him incline his head in acknowledgement. Her fingers had messed up his black hair and as he turned his handsome dark head, stunning golden eyes locking to her as if there were no other person in the world, she felt a fierce pride in his acknowledgement and refused to think beyond that.

As he drove her back to his house she was in a pensive mood and slightly dreamy from the heat, the wine and the passion.

'You're very quiet,' he murmured.

'I thought you would like that.'

In a graceful gesture he linked his fingers briefly with hers. 'No. I miss the chatter, *angelina mia*.'

Zara thought crazily then that engagements could be broken and weddings could be cancelled. That possibility momentarily put paid to the guilt and assuaged her conscience. It had never been her intention to deceive either man but now it was too late to tell Vitale the truth, that she was supposed to be getting married. She shifted uncomfortably at the knowledge that an honest and decent woman would have spoken up much sooner and certainly before the first kiss. Now she could not bear the idea that Vitale might think badly of her and she hugged her secret to herself in silence.

Not surprisingly, with her unusually optimistic mood interspersed by anxious spasms of fear about the future controlling her, the journey back to the farmhouse seemed very short because she was so lost in her thoughts.

She wandered into the sunny hallway. 'I didn't even explore Edith's garden properly,' she remarked with regret.

'Someday I'll take you back to see it,' Vitale promised and then he frowned.

'I'm leaving in the morning,' she reminded him helplessly.

His beautiful dark deep-set eyes lingered on her anxious face and he lifted a hand, brushing her delicate jawbone with his knuckle in an unexpected caress. 'Let your hair down,' he whispered.

The look of anticipation gleaming in his eyes made her heart race and the blood surge hotly through her body. 'Why?' she asked baldly.

'I love your hair…the colour of it, the feel of it,' he confessed huskily.

And like a woman in a dream, Zara lifted her hand and undid the clip. Vitale need no further invitation, angling his proud dark head down as he studied her and used his hands to deftly fluff her rumpled hair round her shoulders. 'I even like the smell of it,' he admitted, a bemused frown tugging at his ebony brows even as his nostrils flared in recognition at the vanilla scent of her.

He was gorgeous, Zara thought dizzily, the most gorgeous guy she had ever met and he seemed equally drawn to her. It was a heady thought, and not her style, but she was basking in the hot golden glow of his appreciative appraisal. It was the work of a moment to mentally douse the sparks of caution at the back of her mind and instead stretch up on tiptoe as if she were free as a bird to do whatever she liked and taste that remarkably beautiful mouth of his again. He lifted her up in his arms and began to carry her upstairs.

CHAPTER FOUR

ZARA surfaced from that kiss to discover that she was on a bed in an unfamiliar room.

It was a larger, more masculine version of her room with bedding the colour of parchment. Unfortunately the last time that Zara had been alone in a bedroom with a man she had been handcuffed half naked to a metal headboard and it was thanks to that terrifying experience that she remained a virgin at the age of twenty-two. Momentarily transfixed by that chilling recollection she turned pale as milk and studied Vitale, reminding herself that she had kissed him, and encouraged him entirely of her own free will. She was not under the influence of alcohol this time around either.

'What's wrong?' His shirt already half unbuttoned to display a dark, hair-roughened wedge of muscular torso, Vitale regarded her with observant eyes, reading her tension and her pallor and wondering at her mood.

He was too clever by half to miss her nervous tension, Zara registered in dismay. A blush of discomfiture warmed her face as she struggled to suppress the apprehension that was a direct result of the betrayal she had suffered. Vitale wasn't a blackmailer, she told herself urgently. He wasn't going to whip out a camera either…at least she hoped not. He was a wealthy successful man in his own right with no need to target her as a potential source of profit.

'It's all right…it's not you,' she told him awkwardly. 'I had a bad experience once…'

Vitale spread his hands in a fluid soothing movement. 'If you want to change your mind I'll understand.'

Her wide eyes prickled with tears at that considerate offer because she knew it could not have been easy for him to make. He was not selfishly putting his own needs first, he *cared* how she felt and that meant a great deal to Zara. After all, in spite of all his protestations Julian had never cared about her, he had only seen her as a means to an end, a convenient conduit to her father's bank account. Her chin came up and she kicked off her shoes in a statement of intent. It was time she shook off the shadows cast over her life by Julian Hurst; it was time that she accepted that not every man was a user or an abuser.

'I'm staying,' Zara informed him unevenly, fighting her nerves with all her might. Twenty-two and a virgin—no, she absolutely was not going to share that embarrassing truth with him. She had read somewhere that men couldn't tell the difference so he would never guess the level of her inexperience unless she made it obvious by parading her insecurity.

Vitale wanted to tell her that she wouldn't regret sharing his bed but he was no hypocrite and he knew that she would. But what was another one-night stand to a woman with her level of experience? Unhappily for him, however, nothing seemed as cut and dried as it had before and he was suffering stabs of indecision directly in conflict with his usual rock-solid assurance and resolute focus. When and how had the business of avenging his sister contrived to become a guilty pleasure?

How could a little pixie-like blonde threaten to come between him and his wits? Vitale always knew what he was doing and controlled his own fate every step of the way. Time after time in his life he had made tough choices and he had never flinched from them. He might loathe the fact but he wanted Monty Blake's daughter much more than he had ever dreamt possible. Even knowing that she was engaged to another man and a heartless little cheat didn't kill his desire for her. Did it matter how he felt though? Surely all that mattered was that he took revenge for his sister's pitiful death at the hands of a filthy coward? And the woman on his bed was the magic key to that much desired objective.

'Take the shorts off,' he urged huskily.

Tensing, Zara was very still for a moment before she scrambled off the bed. It was a modest request, she told herself. He hadn't asked her to take off everything. But she was all fingers and thumbs as she undid the button at the waistband of her shorts and shook her slim hips clear of the garment, finally stepping out of them to reveal a pair of high cut blue satin knickers.

There was something wrong. What, Vitale didn't know, but his instincts were good and he sensed it. Her face was pink, her eyes evasive below concealing lashes and her movements curiously stiff. This was not a woman confident in the bedroom and the suspicion sparked a sense of unease in him for once again she was defying the picture he had of her. Her lavender eyes met his with an unmistakeably anxious glint and her arms were crossed defensively. He recalled that bad experience she had mentioned and wondered just how bad it had been to leave a beautiful young woman so unsure of herself. Disconcerted by the train of his thoughts, Vitale reminded himself that he only wanted to spend the night with her, not step into her mind and psychoanalyse her. He never went deep in relationships, never got involved. He liked his affairs light and easy, with sex the main event and no bitter aftertaste. What was it about her that continually off-balanced him?

Zara had always worried about displaying her body to a man. Unforgettably Julian had laughed at her very slight curves, remarking that she might as well have been a boy as she would never make a centrefold. She had once considered getting a breast enlargement but had feared that with so slim a body she might end up looking top heavy and unnatural. Now all of a sudden she wanted to be perfect—she wanted to be perfect purely for Vitale.

'What *is* it?' he prompted, crossing the floor to grip her taut shoulders.

'I'm feeling horribly shy,' she told him in a rush.

He lifted her off her feet and set her on the side of the bed and then he kissed her, knotting one hand into the soft silky fall of her hair to hold her steady. It was a hungry, demanding kiss, his tongue flicking against the sensitive roof of her mouth to fire a response that raced through her like an explosive depth charge. She forgot who she was, she forgot who he was, she even contrived to forget that she was a virgin. Her palms skated up over the hard muscular wall of his powerful chest and with a groan deep in his throat he caught her hand and, in a stark expression of need, brought it down to the thrust of his erection beneath his trousers.

Pleased to recognise that he wanted her that much, Zara stroked him and struggled to run down his zip. Her slim fingers skimmed beneath the fabric to find the long, thick evidence of his arousal. He pushed against her hand, hard, eager, and hungry for her touch and it fired her up, finally convincing her that in spite of her inexperience she was sexy enough to turn him on hard.

Vitale yanked off her T-shirt with impatient hands and kissed her again while pushing her back across the bed. His urgency, as he dispensed with his trousers while exchanging hard, driving kisses that stoked her hunger higher and higher, was undeniable. He couldn't get enough of her, couldn't get close enough. Zara knew exactly what she wanted for all her lack of experience. She wanted him on top of her, she craved his weight, but instead he found the petal-soft pink tips of her small breasts and used his mouth on those delectable buds with a skill that wrung a gasp from her parted lips.

'You're very sensitive there, *gioia mia*,' Vitale breathed thickly, raking her dainty breasts with eager, admiring eyes.

No longer concerned about the size of her attributes, Zara trembled, insanely conscious of the wet heat building at the heart of her, but for an instant, when he skimmed off his boxers and she saw the powerful upstanding proof of his excitement, her nerves almost betrayed her. Her body craved him but she was afraid it might hurt. Irritated with herself, she suppressed that fear and then all such thoughts fled her mind as he explored her most private place that she was tempted to hide from him. But the desire was too strong, the sensation he gave her too intense to be denied by modesty.

He lay on the bed teasing at her lower lip with tiny little bites that only inflamed her more while he touched her most tender flesh with a skill that made her back arch and her hips lift off the mattress. He eased a finger inside her and groaned against her swollen mouth. 'You're so tight, so wet…'

Her face burned and an ache bloomed between her thighs, an unbearable yearning for much more. With his thumb he found her clitoris and all thought and awareness fell away, reducing her to a much more elemental level. She pushed up to him and kissed him wildly for herself, shivering when the straining buds of her nipples grazed his warm hard chest.

All masculine dominance, Vitale leant over her, dark golden eyes ablaze with desire as he kissed her long and hard. 'I want you so much I'm burning…'

'So what are you waiting for?' Zara urged breathlessly, because he had brought her to an edge of anticipation that was intolerable and without her volition her hips were shifting up to him in tiny needy movements.

He tore the foil off a condom and eased it on while she watched, madly curious about what she had never known but rather apprehensive as well, although she was striving to suppress that feeling. He would fit, of course he would. Nature had designed men and women to fit. He leant over her, strong and sure, and she felt the head of him against her slick, damp entrance. Her body trembled with expectation when he plunged into her.

It hurt and a moan of protest escaped Zara. When he froze, staring down at her, his eyes full of enquiry and confusion, she was mortified.

'Zara?' he began, 'I hurt you. I'm sorry—'

'I don't want to discuss it,' Zara told him hurriedly. She could feel the tension draining away, the pain already receding, and suspected she had made a lot of noise about nothing. 'You can continue…'

It was that prim little command now, in the most inappropriate of circumstances, that nearly sent Vitale into a fit of laughter. With difficulty he restrained his amusement, for her lovely face was a picture of disquiet and embarrassment. 'But I hurt you—'

'Some things are just too private to talk about,' Zara assured him.

'You really want me to continue?' Vitale queried in a strained undertone, wondering why no other woman had ever made him want to laugh as she did.

'You might as well now,' Zara pointed out prosaically, abandoning all hope of receiving much enjoyment from the act now.

Just as she thought that, Vitale sank into her up to the hilt and an erotic thrill sizzled through her like the touch of a firebrand on naked skin. As he began to move she struggled to swallow back a gasp of surprise. She felt truly extraordinary, as if her body were directly attuned to his. A sweet torment of pleasure built as he withdrew and then thrust deep again, jolting a low cry from her. She no longer had the ability to rein back her response. Intense, all-consuming pleasure gripped her and she panted for breath, her urgency rising in exact proportion to her need. Her excitement climbed higher and higher, spiralling through her like a bright light fighting to escape. Then, just when she thought she couldn't bear it any more, she reached a peak and fell apart in an exquisite agony of sensation, eyes opening, lips parting in wonderment as he shuddered over her in the throes of his own climax.

Eyes brilliant with gratification, Vitale claimed her mouth one more time. '*Ebbene*...now then, you amazing woman,' he growled hoarsely. 'That was a worthy continuance.'

Feeling wonderfully at peace, Zara pressed her lips gently against his satin-smooth shoulder. He lifted her wrist and let his tongue glide along the pulse there, making her quiver helplessly. She glanced up at him from below her lashes, recognising that this was a guy who knew every button to push. He kicked back the sheet and got up to stride into the bathroom, and she turned over onto her side, still stunned by the power of what she had experienced in his arms.

The aftermath of that wondrous pleasure was still engulfing her. Great sex, she labelled dizzily, but she wanted more and was already wondering if Vitale planned to continue what they had begun. Or was she just a little weekend distraction? That humiliating possibility had to be considered. After all, theirs had been a chance attraction, rather than a more conventional one. Ironically she had sacrificed so much more to be with him, she recognised ruefully. There was no question of her marrying Sergios Demonides now. Furthermore she could barely believe that she had been so blind to the risk of temptation when she agreed to marry a man she neither loved nor cared for simply to please her parents. How immature and foolish was that? Oh, how much easier life would have been now had she paid more heed to Bee's warnings and told Sergios that she was very sorry but she had changed her mind!

Well, she supposed wryly, a change of heart weeks before the wedding invitations even went out was better than a marriage that failed. No doubt Sergios would be annoyed with her for wasting his time. She had wasted everyone's time and no doubt the cancellation of all the wedding arrangements would cost her parents a great deal of money. She had been very foolish and short-sighted about her own needs. But what was done was done and now everything had changed. There was no going back to the mindset she had cherished before she came to Italy and met Vitale Roccanti. He had blown everything she thought she knew about herself to smithereens. She wanted more from a marriage than Sergios could ever have given her.

'Join me in the shower,' Vitale husked from the doorway.

She slid out of the bed as though he had pulled an invisible piece of elastic that had her attached to one end. Being naked without even the coverage of a sheet or his body was a challenge for her, but already the demeaning memories of what Julian had done to her were being replaced by more positive ones. What went without saying was that she wanted to be with Vitale and felt as though she had waited all her life to feel as strongly about a man as she felt about him. Moreover she was overpoweringly conscious that she was flying back to London in the morning and that then the ball would be in his court as to what—if anything—happened next. There was no way she would chase after him—she had way too much pride for that.

Having finally shed his shirt, Vitale caught her up in the doorway and lifted her high against his lean bronzed body. 'I could easily become accustomed to a woman your size, *gioia mia*. You're so easy to move around!'

A smile as bright as a solar flare lit across her face and all thoughts of the future fled to the back of her mind. Right now she would live for the moment. Why not? She was young, she was, if not technically free, morally free in her own mind to enjoy herself. The only cloud on the horizon was the fact she dared not be honest with Vitale for fear of how her explanation about Sergios might alter and indeed destroy his good impression of her.

The shower was already running and Zara gasped as the cascade of water hit her, then Vitale kissed her and nothing else mattered but the need to get as close to him as possible. He sank his hands below her bottom and hoisted her high so that she could wrap her arms round his neck and kiss him back with passionate fervour. As her fingers moved across his strong back she felt the surprising roughness of his skin there and wondered if he had been in an accident, for she was sure what she was feeling was some sort of scarring. But her curiosity was soon overwhelmed by the heat of his mouth on hers. Just as quickly she discovered that she wanted him again for her nipples instantly pinched into prominent aching beads and the slick heat pooled between her legs again.

'You are so hot you burn me,' Vitale rasped, lowering her back onto the tiles again, his strong erection brushing her stomach.

Shower gel foamed between his hands and he transferred it to her sensitised skin. His expert fingers glided over the pouting mounds of her breasts, lingered over her straining nipples, toying with them before slowly delving lower to graze the most tender bud of all in the most indescribably arousing way. Trembling, she leant against him for support, making no attempt to pretend that she was still in control, surrendering entirely to the tingling, taunting need pulsing through her. With a hungry groan, Vitale hoisted her up against him again and swung round to brace her spine against the tiled wall.

'I can't wait,' he breathed, spreading her thighs and bringing her down on him so that her lush opening sheathed his shaft in a single stunning move.

Hands anchored to her hips, he drove deeper into her and then lifted her to withdraw again before thrusting back into her quivering body again. It was incredibly exciting. She couldn't think, couldn't speak, she just hung onto his broad shoulders for what felt like a wildly exciting roller-coaster ride. At some stage he lifted her out of the shower and laid her down on the floor so that he could continue to pleasure her there with tireless vigour. She writhed in a frenzy of abandon and hit another breathtaking climax that sent her spinning off into the stars.

'Wow…' she whispered weakly in the aftermath, belatedly aware of how hard the floor was below her and how heavy he was.

'That wasn't very well planned,' Vitale breathed abruptly, freeing her from his weight and pulling her up with him.

'Planned?' In a sensual daze, Zara blinked and reached for one of the towels on the rail. 'How… *planned*?'

'I forgot to use a condom. Do you take contraceptive pills?'

Zara froze and looked up at him. His devastatingly handsome face was suddenly very serious. 'No,' she said, the size of the risk they'd just taken slowly dawning on her. 'And I'm about halfway through my cycle.'

'I'll be more careful from now on…I promise,' Vitale asserted, running a fingertip caressingly below her sultry lower lip, swollen from his kisses. 'But I do find you incredibly tempting. You make me dangerously impulsive.'

Meeting the urgent appeal in those stunning golden eyes, Zara could barely put one foot in front of another, never mind think logical thoughts. 'I'm sure I'll be fine,' she muttered, suppressing her concern that she might fall pregnant and thinking that if she took after her mother, who, in spite of her longing for more children, had only ever conceived once in her entire life, she probably had nothing to worry about.

As he turned away to reach for a towel she saw his back and her shocked breath caught in her throat. Line after line of raised scars like welts criss-crossed his long, muscular back and there were little round darker marks as well across his shoulders and spine. 'What on earth happened to your back?' she asked abruptly.

Momentarily, Vitale froze in the act of towelling himself dry and shot her a glance over one broad shoulder. 'Ancient history,' he said dismissively.

And he did not offer to share it.

He pulled on boxers and a shirt to go downstairs with her to raid the fridge. It was Giuseppina's day off but she had left the cabinet packed with goodies. They were both very hungry. He lit a candle on the terrace and they sat eating cold spicy chicken and salad washed down with wine and lively conversation. She wanted to ask him about his back again but was reluctant to snoop. Somehow he manoeuvred her back onto his lap and his hands travelled below her tee to cup her breasts. She stretched back against him, helpless in the grip of her instantaneous hunger and they went back to bed where he made love to her twice more. Afterwards, she lay spent on the bed watching Vitale sleep and feeling ridiculously happy.

Even in the moonlight he had the most amazing bone structure, from his high cheekbones to classic nose and his hard, angular jaw line. She wanted to touch him, trace the winged ebony brows, the sensual firmness of his mouth, but she curled her hands into fists of restraint instead. She was thinking and acting like a teenager, a lovesick teenager, she scolded herself impatiently, deliberately turning away from him and lying back again. Somehow she had never got to play it cool with Vitale the way she usually did with men and that made her feel very insecure. They had bypassed the calm getting-to-know-you phase and plunged straight into meaningful looks and passion. He was as attracted to her as she was to him, she reflected wryly, so at least the spell she was under was a mutual one…

Vitale couldn't sleep. When he woke it was still dark and he reckoned that it was the awareness that he had company that had made him feel uneasy. After all, he always slept alone. He never stayed the night with anyone. He didn't like that kind of closeness. By nature he was a loner and after the childhood he had endured he thought it was hardly surprising that he should be uncomfortable with any form of physical intimacy that went beyond sex. But she was very affectionate, hugging and kissing and snuggling into his lean hard frame. His eyes bleak, he eased away from her, resisting that togetherness. It would soon be over. He couldn't work out why he didn't feel happier about that. But then he had never been given to introspection.

'You should have woken me up sooner!' Zara complained several hours later as she struggled to close the zip on her case.

While Vitale had risen early, he had let her sleep in

and it had been a rush to get dressed and packed ready for the time he had said they had to leave. At first it had pleased her that he was making the effort to personally drive her to the airport, but even the most insensitive woman could not have missed out on noticing how polite and almost distant Vitale seemed to be acting all of a sudden. Zara had never had a one-night stand but it struck her that her vision of how a morning after such a night would feel best described Vitale's behaviour. The awkwardness in the atmosphere was not solely her fault. And maybe she *had* just enjoyed a one night stand, she reasoned painfully, maybe this was it for her and Vitale Roccanti.

What were the chances of him trying to conduct a long-distance relationship with her? Did he even visit London in the course of his work? For the very first time she acknowledged that the odds were that she might never see Vitale again.

Her potential client had become a lover and that could well have destroyed any chance of him seriously considering her for the job.

'Do you still want to see a set of plans for the villa?' she enquired stiffly.

'*Sì*, of course,' Vitale confirmed, shooting her a muted glance, his tension palpable as he swept up her case in a strong hand and carried it downstairs for her.

All Zara's suspicious antennae were on alert. Had Vitale already toyed with the idea of telling her not to bother with the plans? Wouldn't that provide a neat end to a potentially embarrassing situation? *I'm never going to see him again. I'm never ever going to see him again.* The conviction cast a pall over Zara's spirits. She told herself she didn't care, that it didn't matter to her, that a few days ago she had never even heard his name before. And while those thoughts whirled round and round in her mind, pride forced her head higher. With brittle efficiency she discussed arrangements for submitting plans for his inspection while ascertaining the exact level of detail he required. As he seemed to have little to say on that score she was convinced that he would reject the plan, but as Blooming Perfect always charged for putting in a basic design her time would not have been entirely wasted.

His lean, strong face set in forbidding lines, Vitale opened the front door and took her small case out to his car. Standing in the porch, she donned her jacket, her delicate features blank as she fought for composure and blamed herself bitterly for having abandoned her professionalism in the first place. This sense of discomfiture, this sharp sense of loss were the payback for her reckless behaviour.

'Zara…' And as she looked up she was taken aback when Vitale closed his arms round her and bent his head to kiss her, because the way he had been behaving actual physical contact had to have been about the last thing she expected from him.

But in the emotional mood Zara was in, his carnal mouth had only to touch hers for her hands to delve possessively back into his black hair. In fact she held him to her for a split second before she yanked her arms away again and angled her head back, having finally recognised in some disconcertion that he had offered her more of a peck than a passionate embrace.

But even as she released him it seemed all hell broke loose. She stared in shock and flinched at the sight of two men wielding cameras only yards away from them. The men leapt up from crouching positions, clearly having taken photos of Vitale and Zara in each other's arms, and tore off into the trees surrounding the property to speedily disappear from sight.

'Where on earth did they come from? Who are they, for goodness' sake?' Zara demanded angrily. 'Why the heck were they taking pictures of us?'

CHAPTER FIVE

'PAPARAZZI. They must've staked out the house to await their chance.' It was the incredible calm with which Vitale made that explanation that first alerted Zara to the idea that something was badly wrong. He didn't seem surprised by the invasion of their privacy or even particularly bothered by it, which shook her.

'But what on earth for?' Zara queried, marvelling at his seemingly laid-back attitude when everybody she knew in the public eye hated the intrusion of muck-raking journalists into their private lives.

'Obviously you know *why* the paps would find photographing you with another man worth their while,' Vitale countered with a harsh edge to his dark deep drawl, his intonation cold enough to make him sound momentarily like a stranger.

Taken aback by that tone, Zara frowned up at him. 'If they were paps, how would they know I was here with you? *Another* man? What are you saying?'

Vitale quirked a derisive brow, stunning eyes dark as pitch and harder than she had ever seen them. 'Have you forgotten your Greek fiancé? The fact that you're marrying Sergios Demonides this summer? In the light of that, proof of your obvious intimacy with me is more than sufficient to sell a grubby tabloid story for a profit.'

Air rasped in Zara's throat and the muscles there tightened, making it hard for her to catch her breath. She was deeply shaken by the level of his information. 'You *know* about Sergios?'

'Obviously,' Vitale admitted drily.

'We're not engaged,' she said limply, not really even knowing why she was troubling to make that distinction since it was painfully obvious that Vitale Roccanti had already judged her badly for her silence on the score of her marital commitment. 'There was no ring, no engagement…it's not like Sergios and I are in love with each other or anything like that—'

Vitale shifted a silencing hand, his lack of interest patent and like another slap in the face. 'Whatever—'

'No.' Zara refused to be silenced, determined to defend her behaviour as best she could. 'As soon as I got back to London I was planning to tell Sergios that I couldn't go ahead and marry him. I wasn't fooling around behind his back. I'm not like that. I had already decided that I couldn't go ahead and marry him after meeting you—'

'It's immaterial to me—'

'You knew about Sergios and yet you said nothing?' Zara pressed, struggling to understand and not linger on that last lethal statement, for nothing positive could be gained from the words, 'It's immaterial to me.' He didn't care that she was supposedly marrying another man? Didn't care in the slightest? That was a declaration of towering lack of interest that cut her to the quick.

'If you're to make your flight, we have to leave now.' Vitale delivered the reminder without any emotion at all.

'I'll catch a later flight at my own expense,' Zara fielded with a slight shake in her voice. 'I'm more interested right now in finding out what's going on here. I went to bed last night with one guy and this morning it's like I've woken up with his nasty identical twin. If you knew about Sergios why didn't you mention it?'

Vitale resisted a strong urge to ask her why she hadn't mentioned it. Why should he care? She was faithless, pleasure-loving. She meant nothing to him, less than nothing. He breathed in deep and slow, suppressing any hint of an emotional reaction. He was keen to be done with the dialogue and it struck him that honesty was probably the best policy in the circumstances. It would draw an efficient line under their entanglement as nothing else could do. 'I was willing to do whatever I could to ensure that your marriage plans fell through as I believe it will have a detrimental effect on your father's hopes of selling the family hotel group to Demonides.'

Zara was so startled by that explanation that her legs wobbled beneath her and she sank down heavily on the low wall surrounding the shrubbery beside the porch. Her lavender eyes narrowed in bemused concentration when she stared up at him. 'What on earth are you talking about?'

'I set you up,' Vitale volunteered grimly, spelling

out the facts without hesitation. 'From start to finish. Contacting your design firm, bringing you out here—'

In receipt of that admission, Zara had slowly turned white as snow. 'Sleeping with me?' she interrupted jerkily, distaste scissoring through her like a blade. 'Was that part of the set-up? If you wanted Sergios to dump me, ensuring embarrassing pictures of his future bride misbehaving appear in some tabloid rag would be a good start.'

'I thought so too but, believe it or not,' Vitale imparted grittily, 'I had no wish to hurt you personally. Your father has always been my target—'

'My father?' Zara could feel her muscles stiffen in shock as she sat there, spine rigid, feet set as neatly together as a small child told to sit still at church, her hands so tightly clasped together in an effort at self-control that her fingers ached. 'Why would my father have been your target?'

A bleak expression entered his eloquent gaze. 'Sixteen years ago, your father took my sister, Loredana, out on a sailing weekend and when the yacht got into trouble he saved his own skin and left her to drown. She was twenty years old and pregnant with his child.'

In shock at that horrible story, Zara slowly shook her head as though to clear it. Sixteen years ago her father had been divorced from Bee's mother but still a single man. Zara had been born quite a few years before her parents actually wed, but then a wedding ring or indeed a child had never kept the older man faithful. She did actually remember something happening, some kind of an upheaval, which had resulted in rows between her parents… What was it? What had happened? Her smooth brow furrowed. But no, her memory seemed to have packed up and gone home. Sixteen years ago, after all, Zara had only been a child of six. Yet Vitale had still targeted her for something he believed Monty Blake had done to his sister?

'So now you know the truth.'

Her teeth set together so hard that her jaw thrummed in punishment but she did not want to break into impulsive speech. Yes, now she knew that once again a man had made a colossal fool of her. Maybe all the people, including her parents, who had called her dumb were right—she had not had the slightest suspicion of Vitale while he had been executing his charm offensive.

Not until this very morning, at the last possible moment, had she recognised his change of mood and attitude. So what did that say about her? That when it came to men she was criminally stupid and blind and ought not to be let out on her own, she thought painfully. To follow a Julian Hurst with a Vitale Roccanti suggested seriously bad judgement. Twice she had fallen headlong for the flattering approaches of men programmed to hurt and use her for their own purposes. And now she felt as if the bottom had fallen out of her world, as if she had been deserted and left utterly lost in alien territory. This guy, who had shamelessly used and abused her, was the guy she had actually believed she might be falling in love with? That was the lowest blow of all and it decimated her pride.

'Call me a taxi to get me to the airport,' Zara told him curtly.

'There is no need for that.' Vitale flung wide the passenger door as if he expected that she would still scramble into the car like an obedient dog.

The delicate bones of her face prominent below her fine skin, Zara fixed scornful lavender eyes on him and ignored the invitation. 'So you slept with me to try and wreck my Dad's big business deal with Sergios. At least I know what a four letter word of a man you are now,' she breathed. 'You used my business to lure me into a trap, deliberately deceived me, took inexcusable advantage of my trust and stole my virginity—'

'Your *virginity*?' Vitale stressed with incredulous bite. 'You couldn't have been a—'

'I *was*. You were my first lover. I don't sleep around. Were you foolish enough to believe all the rubbish printed about me in newspapers?' Zara demanded fiercely, standing up now, narrow shoulders thrown back as she voiced her feelings without embarrassment. 'Of course now I wish I hadn't slept with you but I'm even more relieved to find out firsthand what an unscrupulous bastard you are, so that I can ensure that I have nothing more to do with you—'

'Zara—'

'No, you listen to me for a change!' Zara told him, interrupting with raw driving determination. 'I didn't do anything to harm you or your sister. I didn't even know you existed until I met you. If you had a problem with my father you should have had the courage and decency to talk to him about it and left me out of it. You had no excuse whatsoever for dragging me into your vengeful attack on him.'

Vitale withstood that verbal onslaught in brooding silence. Perhaps, she thought wildly, he realised that she was entitled to her say.

'Are you getting into the car?' he enquired flatly.

'No, call me a taxi. I wouldn't take a lift off you if I was dying!' Zara flung back at him, stepping forward to reach into the car and yank out her case again with a strength born of pure anger.

Vitale made use of his cell phone. 'The taxi will be here in ten.' He lowered the phone again and studied her. 'Was I truly your first lover?'

Zara used two very rude words to tell him where to go and she shocked him with that succinct retort almost as much as she shocked herself, for she was not in the habit of using that kind of language. At the same time, though, she was not prepared to stand there exchanging further conversation with a man who had deliberately set out to ensnare and hurt her.

'You might as well sit down indoors to wait,' Vitale advised curtly.

Zara shot him a look of loathing and remained where she was. 'You ensured that the paps saw me here with you—that's why you kissed me!' she suddenly realized. Her eyes were full of bitter condemnation and contempt but she was ashamed as well because even though Sergios would not be marrying her now he would surely be embarrassed by that sort of publicity and he had done nothing to deserve that from her.

The truth, Vitale had pronounced, when he told her the story about his sister—was that what it was? She knew there could be many shades of the truth and she doubted his version. Had Monty Blake honestly stood by and let some young pregnant girl drown? It would surprise her if it was true. She didn't like her father and feared him when he was in a temper. He had adored her brother, Tom, the clever son he had longed to see follow in his narcissistic footsteps, but Zara had only ever been a disappointment to him. Her father was obsessed with money and social status. He had a mean amoral streak, a violent temper and a tendency to lash out physically, but he had never done anything, to her knowledge, that suggested he might be downright evil.

It dawned on her then that her father would kill her for getting involved with another man and offending Sergios. Even in the sunshine, a chill of genuine apprehension ran down Zara's taut spine and turned her skin clammy and cold. Only the brave crossed Monty Blake. Her mother would be outraged as well. And Zara would have to avoid Bee to ensure that her half-sister did not get involved in her troubles because her father would go spare if Bee supported her. In fact, Zara recognised painfully, she wasn't going to be anybody's flavour of the month after that photo of her kissing Vitale appeared in print. She might not have been engaged to Sergios, but even without an official announcement lots of people had guessed that a wedding was in the offing.

Vitale watched the taxi disappear down the wooded lane. It was over and, honour satisfied, he could return to his smooth, civilised existence, organising multimillion-euro deals and travelling between the apartments he owned round the world. He had done what he set out to do, smoothly and effectively. He should be pleased that after so many years the only kind of justice that a man of Monty Blake's greed would understand was finally about to be served to him. But impending victory had a strangely hollow and unsatisfying feel.

In his mind's eye the banker renowned for his cold calculation and emotional detachment could still see Zara Blake's pale heart-shaped face and the incredulity etched in her eyes. In a sudden movement he punched the wall with a clenched fist. It was a crazy thing to do and he was not a man who did crazy things and it hurt like the very devil. Blood from his bruised and scraped knuckles dripped on the tiled floor but that aberrant surge of violence did serve to vent a little of the raging sense of frustration Vitale was struggling to suppress. He had no idea why he felt this way.

Had Zara been a virgin? He saw no reason for her to lie on that score and he had only dismissed the suspicion because it had seemed so unlikely that a rich and beautiful party girl could still be that innocent at her age. He recalled her lack of assurance in the bedroom and his wide, shapely mouth twisted as he acknowledged that he *had* been guilty of believing what he had read in the media about her. Few party girls were virgins, but she had been and he had ignored his suspicion precisely because it had suited him to do so. Had he known the truth about Monty Blake's daughter would he still have used her as a weapon to strike at her father? He could not answer that question. He still wondered why there had been no man before him and then he shook his head, killing the thought as well as that dangerous seed of burning curiosity. It was done and there was no going back. Now he only had to wait for Demonides to ditch the buyout of the Royale hotel group at an inflated price and he would have achieved his final goal.

Even so, for the very first time Vitale was tentatively questioning the desire for revenge that had driven him since the age of thirteen. It was like probing a ragingly sensitive tooth. As a boy he had known it would be a foolish waste of time to stage a personal confrontation with his sister's former lover. Monty Blake would simply lie to him as he had lied at the inquest. He was a vain and devious man, not to be trusted with women. Vitale shut out the reflection that the end might not always justify the means. He had done what had needed to be done. The scornful condemnation in those amazing lavender eyes could not destroy the painful memories of his innocent and trusting sister or his powerful need to hit back on her behalf. Loredana hadn't been a 'someone'. She had had no powerful connections—at least, Vitale adjusted grimly, none who *cared* enough to question the judgement of accidental death made at that inquest.

In comparison, Zara Blake meant nothing to him, less than nothing, he affirmed with vigour. He was not an emotional man. In all likelihood he would never see her again. Unless she proved to be pregnant, he thought abruptly, and, after what he had done, wouldn't that be a disaster to end all disasters? He still could not credit that he could have taken that risk with her. Since when had sex been so overwhelming an event? He had always been proud of his self-control, not a trait that came naturally to those of his bloodline, he conceded grimly. So, how could passion have betrayed him to that extent? In truth it had been an extraordinary weekend—Zara had defied his expectations at every turn and precious little had gone according to plan.

But why was he questioning his behaviour? Why the hell had he smashed his fist into a wall? He was a goal-orientated man and, having achieved his objective, he ought to be celebrating. After all, Demonides was never going to go ahead and marry Zara Blake once he saw that photo of her in another man's arms in the newspapers. Vitale decided that the problem was that he had got too close to his quarry. He had found her intensely desirable and quite impossible to resist, and all that was wrong was that the shock of that was still ricocheting through a man who rated his strength of mind and self-discipline as exceptional.

'Ignore them, darling,' Jono advised Zara in a tone of crisp dismissal as he helped her stack another box in the van he had borrowed to help her move into her new home. Fluffy was peering out of her carrier, little round eyes full of anxiety. The rabbit hated change and travel of any kind.

A pair of enormous sunglasses anchored on her nose, Zara endeavoured to look indifferent to the pair of reporters shouting rude questions while taking photos to record her departure from her parents' elegant town house. If only she had moved out and embraced independence long ago, she reflected ruefully, she wouldn't be feeling quite so lost. On the other hand, every cloud had a silver lining. This was the first day of her new life, she reminded herself bracingly. Her parents might have thrown their troublesome daughter out and washed their hands of her, but at least she was now free to do as she liked and concentrate on Blooming Perfect.

Jono glanced at Zara's tense profile before he drove off and squeezed her hand in a comforting gesture. 'Things will get better once you can settle into your new flat.'

'They could hardly get worse.' Blond and blue-eyed, Jono, a successful PR consultant, was one of the few friends who had stuck by Zara when the proverbial had hit the fan ten days earlier.

As a well-known socialite and the rumoured future bride of one of the world's wealthiest men, Zara had been extremely popular. Stripped of her father's money and the luxury lifestyle that had accompanied it, she had learned that she was more of an acquired taste in the friendship stakes. She would no longer be able to afford the shopping expeditions, the trips abroad or the expensive pastimes that she had once taken for granted. Of course, given the chance Bee would have stood by her side, but Zara had been determined not to enrage her father even more by encouraging her half-sister to get involved in her problems.

After all, Zara accepted that she had made some very bad decisions and it was the way of the world that she should have to pay the price for her mistakes. That photo of her with Vitale after spending the week-end with him in what had been gruesomely described as a 'love nest in the Tuscan hills' had appeared in one of the murkier tabloids. Sergios had wasted little time in cutting her loose. Her former bridegroom's phone call, Zara recalled with a cringing sense of mortification, had been a masterpiece of icy restraint. Sergios had not reproached or condemned her, he had merely pointed out that it was obvious that they would not suit and that had been that. He had rung off while she was still stuck like a record in a groove trying to apologise for the sort of scandal and behaviour that no woman could adequately apologise for.

In comparison to Sergios' moderation, her parents' fury had known no bounds. Things had been hurled in vicious verbal onslaughts that had almost inevitably led to Monty Blake's raging demand that his daughter move out from below his roof. But, she acknowledged ruefully, at least her enraged father had confined himself to vocal abuse and retained some shred of control over his temper. Sadly that was not always the case.

She had done a search on the Net in an effort to dig up the story of her father and the yacht episode. The sparse facts available had left her none the wiser when it came to apportioning blame. An Asian earthquake and the resulting waves had caused the hired yacht to sink in the middle of the night. Apparently it had happened very quickly. One member of the crew and a passenger called Loredana, described as an Italian fashion model, had been listed missing, presumed drowned. When her father was already furious she had seen little point in mentioning an incident that would only madden him even more. Furthermore, if even an inquest had failed to extract any damaging admission of culpability from the older man she had little faith in the likelihood of her own persuasive powers doing a better job. And why wasn't she being more honest with herself? She had not brought up that business with the yacht because she was frightened of pushing her father's temper over the edge. No, she had been too much of a coward.

The studio apartment she had rented was a masterpiece of clever design in which the minimum possible space was stretched to cover the essentials but it covered nothing well, Zara conceded ruefully as she unpacked, aghast at the lack of storage space. If there was little room for the requirements of ordinary life, there was even less for Fluffy. A neighbour had already informed Zara that no pets were allowed in the building and had threatened to report her to the landlord. Just then that seemed to be the least of Zara's worries, though. By the time she had finished shopping for bed linen, food and kitchen necessities, the balance in her bank account had shrunk alarmingly. Bearing in mind that she had only the small salary she could draw from her late aunt's business, she would have to learn to do without things if she didn't want to run into debt. Now that she was in a position to work full-time it would have suited her to dispense with Rob's services as manager, but, owing to Zara's dyslexia and the restrictions it imposed, Rob had become an essential component in the successful running of the business.

She went to bed early on her first night in the apartment. The instant she closed her eyes in a silence disturbed only by the sounds of traffic the anguish she had fought off to the best of her ability all day flooded back: the intense sense of loss and betrayal, the conviction that she had to be the most stupid woman ever born, the swelling, wounding ache of deep hurt. And she walled up that giant mess of turmoil and self-loathing, shut it out and reminded herself that tomorrow was another day.

That same week in his Florence head office, Vitale's oft-admired powers of concentration let him down repeatedly in meetings when his mind would drift and his shrewd dark eyes would steadily lose their usual needle-sharp focus. The teasing image of a tiny blonde haunted his sleep and shadowed his working hours with unfamiliar introspection. By night he dreamt of Zara Blake in all sorts of erotic scenarios doing all sorts of highly arousing things to his insatiable body. Evidently with her in a starring role his imagination took flight.

Even a resolute procession of cold showers failed to chase the pain of his constant lingering arousal and, being innately practical, he immediately sought a more effective solution to his overactive libido. Since Zara had returned to the UK he had dined out with two different women, taken another to the opera and accompanied a fourth to a charity event. All were extremely attractive and entertaining. Any one of them would have slept with him without attaching strings to the occasion, but not one of those women had tempted him and for the first time he had found himself actively avoiding intimate situations. He had also discovered flaws in all four women and now asked himself when he had become so very hard to please. But while he loathed constant female chatter one of the women had proved too quiet, another had had a very irritating laugh, the third had talked incessantly about shopping and the fourth had constantly searched out her own reflection in mirrors.

Every day Vitale had all the key English newspapers delivered to his office and he skimmed through them mid-morning over his coffee without once admitting to himself what he was actually on the lookout for. Yet every day he contrived to take his coffee break just a little earlier. During the second week, however, he finally hit the jackpot when he saw the photo of Zara with another man. He frowned, at first wondering who the good-looking blond male by her side was. She looked tinier than ever pictured with a suitcase almost as big as she was. He read between the lines of the gossip column below. Her family was angry enough with her to throw her out of their home? What else was he supposed to think?

Vitale was very much shocked, mentally picturing a puppy being dumped at the side of a busy motorway, a puppy with no notion of how to avoid the car wheels racing past. Monty Blake's daughter, surely spoiled and indulged all her life to date, could have few survival skills to fall back on. Honed to a cutting edge by a very much tougher background and much more humble beginnings, Vitale was appalled on her behalf. He had not foreseen such a far-reaching consequence but he felt that he should have done. After all, the loss of Sergios Demonides as a son-in-law would have been a major disappointment and Monty Blake was not the type of man to deal gracefully with such a setback. Evidently he had taken his ire out on his only child.

Feeling disturbingly responsible for that development, Vitale lifted the phone and organised a flight to London in his private jet that evening. He only wanted to check that she was all right, that was all, nothing more complex, certainly nothing personal, although if she turned out to have conceived, he conceded broodingly, matters would swiftly become a great deal more personal. Vitale, after all, knew that he would be the last man alive to take a casual approach to an unplanned pregnancy. He knew too well the potential drawbacks of such a route. It took another couple of phone calls to establish where Zara was staying and the unwelcome gossip he received along with that information persuaded him that Monty Blake's daughter must be having a pretty tough time.

But why should that matter to him? Vitale frowned heavily, deeply ill-at-ease with his reactions. Why did he feel so accountable for what might happen to her? While Vitale was, at least, a free agent Zara had chosen to betray the trust of the man she had promised to marry. She was a faithless liar without a conscience, the spoilt daughter of a man he loathed. But he still could not shake the recollection that he had been Zara's one and only lover. The reflection that he had been wrong about her on that score made him wonder whether there could be other things he might have been wrong about as well. And for a man as self-assured as he was that was a ground-breaking shift in outlook.

The next day, Vitale called at Zara's apartment at

nine in the morning. Even before he entered the building he was asking himself why the hell he was making a social call on the daughter of his enemy. He might have got her pregnant, he reminded himself with fierce reluctance, his handsome mouth down curving. If there was a child he had a duty of care towards her and until he knew one way or the other he could not turn his back on her and ignore her predicament. Born into a comfortable background, she had enjoyed a sheltered upbringing, so how was she coping without that safety net?

Vitale stepped out of the lift on Zara's floor and right into a heated dispute. A burly older man was standing at Zara's front door saying aggressively, 'This isn't open to negotiation—either the rabbit goes or you move out!'

Zara gave him a stricken look. 'But that's—'

'No pets of any kind. You signed the rent agreement and you're in breach of the conditions,' he pronounced loudly. 'I want that animal out of here today or I'm giving you notice to quit.'

'I don't have anywhere else to take her,' Zara was arguing heatedly.

'Not my problem,' the landlord told her, swinging on his heel and striding into the lift that Vitale had only just vacated.

Only as Vitale moved forward did Zara register his presence and her eyes flew wide, her lips parting in furious surprise and dismay. 'What the hell are you doing here?'

CHAPTER SIX

AT first glimpse of Vitale, shock shrouded Zara like a cocoon, so that external sounds seemed to come from a very long way away. The traffic noise, the doors opening and closing in the busy life of the building faded fast into the background. As her landlord stomped angrily away, offended by her combative stance, Vitale took his place. Even at a glance, Vitale looked fabulously, irretrievably Italian in a faultlessly cut grey business suit that had that unmistakeable edge of designer style. From his cropped black hair and staggeringly good bone structure to his tall, well-built body, he was a breathtakingly handsome man.

But it hurt to look at him, and as Zara felt the pain of his deception afresh her anger ignited like a roaring flame. Her eyes cloaked, hiding her vulnerability. He hadn't cared about her, hadn't even really wanted her for herself. He had simply used her as a weapon to strike at her father. 'What do you want?' she asked, her intonation sharp with anger. 'And how did you find out where I was living?'

'I have my sources,' Vitale fielded, his stunning dark deep-set eyes trained on her to track any changes.

Casually clad in cropped trousers and flip-flops, she seemed smaller and younger than he had recalled but, if anything, even more beautiful. Her creamy natural skin was flawless. The wealth of silvery waves falling round her narrow shoulders was bright as a beacon, providing the perfect frame for delicate features dominated by wide lavender eyes and an impossibly full and tempting pink mouth. And that fast Vitale wanted her again. The tightening heaviness at his groin was a response that unnerved him more than a little. He operated very much on cold, clever logic—he had no time and even less understanding of anything uncontrolled or foolish. He could not compute the sheer irrational absurdity of such an attraction when he had remained indifferent to so many more suitable women. In self-defence, he immediately sought out her flaws. She was *too* small, her hair was *too* bright, she talked like an express train rarely pausing for breath and much of it was totally superfluous stuff. But in defiance of popular report, he recalled abstractedly, she was anything but stupid. She had a quirky sense of humour and very quick wits.

While Vitale looked her up and down as though he had every right to do so, his face sardonic and uninformative, Zara's resentment merely took on a sharper edge. 'You still haven't told me what you're doing here.' Her heart-shaped face had tightened, irate colour stealing into her cheeks as she belatedly grasped the most likely reason for his reappearance, and she winced in discomfiture. 'Oh, of course, you want to know *if*—'

'May I come in?' Vitale incised, not being a fan of holding intimate conversations in public places.

'I don't want to let you in but I suppose I don't have much choice,' Zara countered ungraciously, reflecting that far from worrying about the possibility of an accidental pregnancy she had shelved the concern in Italy and had refused to think about it again when it seemed that she had so many more pressing things to worry about.

A thumping noise broke the tense silence. At Vitale's entrance, Fluffy thumped the floor with her hind feet in protest and let out a squeal of fright before hotfooting it for her hutch.

Vitale was even more taken aback by the display. 'You keep a…rabbit indoors?' he queried, his only prior experience of rabbits being the belief that people either shot them or ate them and sometimes both.

'Yes, Fluffy's my pet. She's nervous of men,' Zara remarked, wishing she had been as sensibly wary as Fluffy when she had first met him, for it might have protected her from harm.

Indeed in a rage of antipathy, she was looking fixedly at Vitale. Somehow she couldn't stop looking and all of a sudden and without the smallest warning she was recalling much more of that night in the love nest in the Tuscan hills than was necessary or decent. She remembered the early morning light gleaming over the black density of his tousled hair. She had run her fingers through that hair before she ran them over the corrugated flatness of his incredibly muscular torso and traced the silken length of his shaft, exploring him in a way she had never wanted or needed to explore any other man. Her heart was beating so fast in remembrance of those intimacies that she wanted to press a hand against it to slow it down before it banged so hard it burst loose from her chest.

'I don't know if I'm pregnant or not yet,' she admitted frankly, descending straight to the prosaic in the hope of bringing herself back down to planet earth again, safe from such dangerous mental wanderings. He might be gorgeous but he was her enemy and a callous con artist and she hated him for what he had done to her.

Still disconcerted by the presence of a bunny rabbit whose quivering nose was poking out of the elaborate hutch, Vitale frowned, uneasy with a situation he had never been in before. The sort of lovers he usually had took precautions and accidents didn't happen, or at least if they did they were kept quiet, he acknowledged cynically. 'I believe there are tests you can do.'

'I'll buy one and let you know the result when I've done it,' she muttered carelessly. 'But right now I've got more important things to worry about—'

Vitale raised a brow. 'Such as…what exactly?'

'Fluffy, my pet rabbit—what am I going to do with her? My neighbour has already lodged a complaint and you heard the landlord! He wouldn't budge an inch. He's going to chuck me out of here if I don't rehome Fluffy!' she exclaimed.

'Rules are rules,' Vitale pronounced, a little out of

his depth when it came to keeping pets because he had never had one of any kind. It was a challenge for him to understand the depth of her attachment to the animal, but her distraught expression did get the message across. Growing exasperation gripped him. 'Perhaps you could give the rabbit away.'

Zara dealt him a furious look of condemnation. 'I couldn't give Fluffy away!' she gasped. 'She's been with me since my sixteenth birthday and I love her. Thanks to you I've been put through an awful lot of grief over the last couple of weeks but I can cope with it because I'm strong.'

Vitale was still very much focused on what was most important to him and detached from the rabbit scenario. 'I'll buy you a pregnancy test and bring it back here—'

'Don't put yourself out!' Zara slung him a seething look of hatred that startled him, for he had not appreciated that those lavender eyes could telegraph that amount of aversion.

Vitale compressed his sensual mouth and heaved a sigh. 'I must. I'm equally involved in this situation and I can't relax until we have found out where we stand.'

'Well, if wondering about where you stand is all you're worrying about I can help you right now!' Zara fired back at him. 'I hate you. If I find out I'm pregnant, I'll hate you even more. What will I do? I'll trail you through every court in the land for financial support and I'll hope it embarrasses the hell out of you!'

Vitale dealt her a seething look of impatience. 'If you are pregnant you won't have to trail me through a court for financial support. I would pick up the bills without argument.'

Unimpressed by that declaration and cringing at the unhappy thought of being beholden to him, Zara stood so straight her spine ached and her eyes glowed like embers in a banked down fire. 'Then I'll fight *not* to accept your financial support!' she slung back.

Vitale was not slow on the uptake and he got the message that whatever it took she was currently out for his blood. As there was nothing that whet his appetite more than a challenge, a sardonic smile slashed his wonderfully well-shaped mouth. She didn't know who she was dealing with. 'I'll be back soon,' he warned her before he turned on his heel.

'You're not the Terminator,' she told his back acidly before the lift doors closed on him.

Vitale, her sleek sophisticated banker, had gone to buy her a pregnancy test, surely a humble task beneath his high-powered notice? He was not hers, she scolded herself angrily, marvelling that such a designation had even occurred to her. Why was she even speaking to him? Her period was already four days late, a fact she had kept pushed to the back of her mind because she already had more than she could handle on her plate. Usually, however, she was as regular as clockwork in that department, so her disrupted cycle was a source of concern. She stroked Fluffy, inwardly admitting that she really didn't want to do a test yet because she much preferred to keep her spirits up by concentrating on sunnier prospects. My goodness, she reflected with a creeping feeling of apprehension, becoming a single parent in her current circumstances would be a nightmare.

Within the hour, Vitale returned and handed her a carrier bag. Zara extracted, not one, but four different boxes containing pregnancy-testing kits.

'I had no idea which you would prefer,' Vitale declared without a shade of discomfiture. Zara dug into the biggest box and extracted the instructions. The print was so tiny she couldn't read it and the diagram just blurred. Her hand shook, a sense of intense humiliation threatening to eat her alive and turning her skin clammy with perspiration. 'Go home,' she told him shakily.

'Why? I might as well wait.' Vitale's impatience to know the result was etched on his face and hummed from his taut restive stance. He lifted one of the other boxes. 'Use that one. From what I read on the box I understand it can give an immediate result.'

Grateful for that information, Zara took it and unwrapped it, spreading out the instructions on the table with a careful hand, squinting down at it as calmly as she could in an unsuccessful attempt to focus on the minuscule print. All she could see was a blur of mismatched symbols. She thought it was most probably her mood and the awful awareness that she had an audience that was making her dyslexia even worse than it usually was. She needed to stay calm and focused but just at that instant her self-discipline was absent.

'What's wrong?' Vitale queried rather curtly.

Zara breathed in slow and deep. 'The print is so small I can't read it,' she complained.

Assuming that she had imperfect sight but was not

prepared to own up to the fact or indeed have anything done about it, Vitale suppressed a groan and lifted the sheet to read the relevant sentences. Zara would have much preferred to have read it herself. Her cheeks flared red and hot but, veiling her gaze, she made no comment. As she locked herself into the tiny shower room with the kit she thought that anything was better than him discovering the truth about her affliction.

Only when Zara reached sixth form had a concerned teacher asked her mother to allow an educational psychologist to test her daughter. Identified as severely dyslexic, Zara had finally been offered the assistance that she needed to catch up with her peers. Unfortunately by that stage her self-esteem had sunk to rock-bottom and she had been unable to believe that reasonable exam grades might be within her reach. Her father, after all, had immediately dismissed her dyslexia as a 'poor excuse for stupidity' and had refused to credit the existence of such a condition.

Although a speech-language therapist had been recommended to teach Zara how to handle the problem, her father had refused to consider that option, saying it would be a waste of time and money. Unsurprisingly Zara had never recovered from her father's shame and disgust at the news that his daughter suffered from something labelled 'a learning disability'. It was a subject never ever mentioned in her home but she often suspected it was the main reason why her parents continued to look on her as some sort of perpetual child, rather than the adult that she was.

Zara stood in the shower room with her attention on

the novelty wall clock left behind by a previous tenant, refusing to allow herself to simply stare at the test to see if it had changed colour. The waiting time up, she straightened her shoulders and finally directed her gaze to the tiny viewing window on the test wand and there was the line of confirmation that she had most feared to see. Her legs almost buckled beneath her and she broke out in a cold sweat of horror.

Wrenching open the door, Zara reeled out. 'It's bad news, I'm afraid,' she proclaimed jaggedly.

'Let me see.' Accustomed to trusting in only his own powers of observation, Vitale insisted on checking the test. He might have paled had his attention not been on Zara, who was displaying more than enough shock and consternation for both of them.

'You can leave now,' she told him woodenly.

But Vitale stayed where he was, his attention involuntarily fixing to her flat stomach. A baby, she was going to have *his* baby. He was going to have a child with Monty Blake's daughter. He was utterly appalled at the news. A selfish moment of inattention in the heat of passion was all it had taken to permanently change both their lives. Yet he more than anyone had known the potential cost of such negligence and had the least excuse for the oversight, he conceded with stormy self-loathing.

'I can't simply leave you like this,' Vitale declared with a harsh edge to his deep drawl.

'Why not?' Zara gave him a deadened look, still too traumatised to think beyond what she had just learned about her own body. 'Don't you think you've already done enough?'

In the face of that unnecessary reminder, Vitale stood his ground. It was a bad moment but in almost thirty years he had lived through an awful lot of bad moments and he would not allow himself to flinch from anything unpleasant. But for him the worst aspect was that this was an event outside his control and he liked that reality least of all. 'I'd like to deal with this before I leave.'

Zara folded her arms and lifted her chin, suspicious of that particular choice of wording. '*Deal* with it?' she questioned, astonished by the current of protectiveness towards her unborn child that sprang into being inside her and stiffened every defensive muscle. 'I should tell you now—I'm not prepared to have a termination—'

'I'm not asking you to consider that option,' Vitale countered, exasperated by her drama, craving a sensible solution even though he already knew there probably wasn't one. 'You don't trust me but I assure you that I will only act in my child's best interests.'

Zara was unimpressed. How could she trust anything he said? How did she know that getting her pregnant hadn't been part of his revenge? Hadn't he accused her father of getting his sister pregnant? How much faith could she put in Vitale's promises now?

'That's quite a sudden change of attitude you've had,' she remarked in a brittle voice.

His lips set in a firm line, his eyes flaring bright and forceful before he cloaked them. Even though she tried not to, she found herself staring because, regardless of her hatred and distrust, nothing could alter the reality that he was sleek and dark and beautiful as sin.

'Whether I like it or not the fact that you're going to have my child does change everything between us,' he responded darkly.

Zara released a tart laugh of disagreement. 'Even though you believe that my father is the equivalent of a murderer and hate me for being his daughter?'

Anger lent a feverish hint of colour to his exotic high cheekbones and gave Vitale's appearence such striking strength and magnetism. 'I do *not* hate you.'

Scorn crossed Zara's heart-shaped face. 'You're not being honest with yourself. You hate me for the blood that runs in my veins. How else could you think it was acceptable to treat me so badly?'

Vitale did not think in the emotive terms that came so naturally to her. He was in a stormy mood, naturally resentful of the predicament they were in, but still logical enough to accept that anger would do nothing to solve the problems they faced. He saw even less sense in harking back to the past. 'The day we learn that you are carrying my baby is not the time to discuss such issues,' he told flatly. 'We have more important matters to consider—'

'The fact that I hate and distrust you tends to overpower every other impression,' Zara shot back at him, furious at being targeted by that superior little speech and wishing that she knew exactly what he was thinking. Unfortunately that lean darkly handsome face was uniquely uninformative.

'At the very least I would ask you to see a doctor for a check-up as soon as possible,' Vitale advised.

'When I can find the time.' Zara glanced at her watch. 'You really do have to leave. I have an appointment with a client in an hour and I'm not even dressed yet! Oh, my goodness, I forgot, what am I going to do about Fluffy?'

Vitale's sculpted lips parted. 'I'll take her,' he said, startling himself with that announcement almost as much as he startled his companion.

'Are you serious?' Zara stared back at him in stunned disbelief.

'Why not?' Having made the offer, Vitale refused to back down from the challenge. She had quite sufficient thoughts to occupy her without stressing about her pet's impending homelessness. She needed peace of mind to concentrate on her own condition and if removing the wretched rabbit could deliver that he was willing to take care of the problem for her.

'You can't give her away to someone, you know,' she warned him doubtfully. 'Or have her put down or anything like that.'

Vitale dealt her a grimly comprehensive scrutiny, now fully acquainted with how low she feared he might sink even when it came to a dumb animal. 'In this instance you can be confident that your pet will enjoy the best of care.'

Zara frowned, glancing worriedly at the little animal. 'You're not planning to just dump her in a pet-care place, are you? They're always full of dogs and she's terrified of dogs.'

As that was exactly what Vitale had planned to do with Fluffy, it was a tribute to his ability to think fast that he didn't betray a shred of discomfiture. 'Of course not,' he insisted as though such a thought had not even occurred to him.

Vitale then learned a great deal more than he ever cared to know about bunny rabbits. Fluffy did not travel light either. Even with Zara helping it took two trips down to his car to transport all Fluffy's possessions.

'I'll look after her,' he asserted, challenged to retain his patience.

'I'll need your phone number,' Zara told him. 'I'll ring you later to see how you're getting on.'

If ever there was a moment when an unprecedented attack of benevolence on his part had paid off this was it, Vitale recognised with fearless self-honesty. Ironically the mother of his unborn child was more concerned about her pet than about herself, but an avenue of communication had at least opened again. He was going to be a father. The shock of that thought suddenly engulfed Vitale like an avalanche. A baby, he was thinking in a daze of lingering horror as he installed Fluffy in her three deck condo in the corner of his open plan lounge. The brightly coloured plastic rabbit version of a palace with all mod cons looked incongruous against his elegant décor.

On learning that the rabbit was there to stay for the foreseeable future, Vitale's part-time housekeeper told him thinly that she was allergic to animal fur, and when he failed to offer an immediate solution she handed in her notice on the spot. Zara phoned briefly just to tell

Vitale that Fluffy liked MTV for company, apparently being a bunny with a musical bent.

'Tough luck, Fluff,' Vitale breathed, switching on the business channel to catch the most recent stock figures. 'The guy with the remote calls all the shots.'

Fluffy sidled into view like a bunny with a very good idea of how welcome a house guest she was. She slunk along the skirting and then settled down happily to munch at the corner of a very expensive rug. As Vitale rose to intervene and Fluffy took fright at the movement and fled back to her condo it occurred to him that a young child would, at times, be equally trying to his reserves of patience.

That was, if Zara Blake *allowed* him anywhere near their child. His blood ran cold with apprehension as he pictured that possible scenario of parental powerlessness. He cursed the situation he was in. He had several good friends supporting children they rarely, if ever, saw. He knew that a child's mother generally controlled how much access a father might receive and he was well aware that some mothers preferred not to share. As an unmarried father he would have virtually no rights at all over his own flesh and blood. Vitale had been the son of an unstable mother and the defenceless victim of an abusive stepfather. That he might have little say in his own child's upbringing was a prospect that Vitale could not bear to contemplate. How would he ever be able to protect his child from the risk of abuse? His appetite for work suddenly abating, Vitale shut down his laptop. He fed Fluffy, who had the fine taste of a gourmand, and then he paced the floor to consider his options with a new driving urgency.

In the meantime, Zara was having a very busy day. She spent an hour chatting to a potential client before checking out the current job that Blooming Perfect was engaged in and finally returning to the firm's office to finish a plan.

'It really is quite something,' Rob remarked when he saw the plan she had completed for the villa in Italy.

Zara smiled as she rolled it up and slotted it into a protective cardboard tube. 'Well, we'll see.'

'When will the client get it?'

'This week. He's staying in London.'

'Convenient,' Rob commented, already engaged in closing up for the night.

Only as she drove back to her new apartment and struggled to find a parking spot was Zara at long last free to think of the tiny seed of life growing inside her. A baby, *her* baby. She could still hardly believe it was true and could not suppress a sense of wonderment over the conception that embarrassed her. After all, she could hardly celebrate falling pregnant by a man with whom she no longer had a relationship. That was very bad news for her child. Or was it? Thinking about her own father, Zara was not sure that she had ever enjoyed a single advantage from his presence in her life and he was a fearsome man in a temper. On the other hand she had friends who adored their fathers and found them very supportive and good at giving advice, she conceded fairly.

Her unplanned pregnancy would also give her parents yet another reason to criticise her, although they would have fewer grounds than most to complain, because Zara and her brother had been eight years old before their parents even moved in together. Certainly her father had been in no hurry to commit to the mother of his twins. Indeed even at that point Monty Blake must already have been involved with her sister Tawny's mother.

But Zara was not like either of her parents and she told herself that there was no reason why she shouldn't make a good single mother. As she had no trust fund to fall back on she was lucky to have Edith's business to help her survive on the financial front. She was strong and sensible. In a crisis she would bend, not break, and she was willing to make the best of things. So, she had been more than a little foolish over Vitale? She just had to learn to live with that as he was no doubt learning to live with Fluffy. The serious expression on Zara's face slid away and she almost smiled at that incongruous image. Now that offer of his to look after her pet had come as an enormous surprise. But then Vitale was deep, so deep and complex that she couldn't fathom him and she quite understood how she had been taken in by him. Vitale did not wear his true and tricky nature on the surface.

As she was wondering what to make for her evening meal her cell phone beeped with a text.

Join me for dinner? I'll cook. V

No, absolutely not, Zara thought in dismay and annoyance. What was he playing at? And then a more responsible inner voice reminded her that she was set to have a relationship with Vitale through her child that would stretch quite a few years into her future. Ignoring him, refusing to see him or speak to him might be tempting, but it would not be the sensible path to follow. Sadly, on one issue Vitale was correct. Her pregnancy did mean that everything had changed, although her feelings towards him hadn't changed in the slightest: she still hated him like poison. Bolstered by that conviction, Zara texted back her agreement. After all, meeting up with Vitale would also provide her with an easy way of delivering the plan for the grounds of the Italian villa.

CHAPTER SEVEN

FLUFFY was watching television on the leather sofa when Vitale returned to his apartment that evening. He wouldn't have believed it if he hadn't seen it with his own eyes: the wretched bunny was watching music videos while basking in the comfort of a well-upholstered seat! But no sooner did Zara's pet hear the noise of the front door closing than it raced like a furry streak for the safety of its home in the corner. And there, in spite of the food Vitale brought it, the rabbit stayed firmly out of sight.

But Fluffy had not spent an entirely lazy day, Vitale noted grimly, because the rug had been chewed and the wooden foot of a coffee table had been gnawed. It was a destructive bunny rabbit, utterly unsuited to civilised life in a luxury apartment. On the other hand, Zara had agreed to come to dinner, most probably because she wanted to see how her pet was doing.

The plan for the villa tucked below one arm, Zara arrived sporting an ice-blue dress teamed with incredibly high heels. The pale shade accentuated her eyes and her hair shimmered round her shoulders. For the first time ever Vitale admired a woman's legs and then, quite unnervingly for him, thought of her safety instead. What if she stumbled and fell and got hurt?

'Those shoes are like stilts,' he remarked before he could think better of the comment, only to watch in amazement as Fluffy bounded out into the hall to greet her mistress and gambol round her feet in a welcoming display.

Zara petted Fluffy and talked to her. Anything was better than focusing on Vitale, breathtakingly handsome even casually clad in jeans and an open-necked black shirt. She decided that she was horrendously overdressed and felt as though she had lost face in some secret contest of who could act the most laid-back. Her heart was doing that bang-bang-bang thing again but that was just the natural effect of Vitale's manifold attractions hitting her defences with all the subtlety of a ten-ton truck.

He served the meal immediately in the spacious dining annexe off the lounge. He had made steak and salad, nothing fancy, but she was impressed all the same, her one and only attempt to cook steak having resulted in a lump of tough and rubbery meat that nobody could eat. The silence stretching between them seemed to shout in her ears, reminding her with a painful pang of regret how easily they had once talked in Italy. That, of course, she recalled, had only been part and parcel of his deception.

'How do you feel?' Vitale asked her levelly.

'Like I'm stuck inside a soap bubble. The baby

doesn't really feel real yet, probably because it's such an unexpected development,' she admitted.

'I intend to give you all the support that I can.'

At that austere unemotional promise, a tight little smile formed on Zara's lips. 'Then give me space.'

Space was the very last thing Vitale could imagine offering her at that moment. In one of those infuriating shifts of awareness that infiltrated his formidable calm a surge of heat consumed him as he focused on her luscious mouth and recalled what she could do with it. Subjected to an instant erection, Vitale breathed in deep and slow, furiously willing his undisciplined body back under control and deeply resentful of the effect she could have on him. 'I don't think I can do that. I feel responsible for you now.'

Her eyes were cool and flat as glass. 'But that's not how I feel and not what I want.'

'Don't make our child pay the price for what I did in Italy,' he urged her forcefully, already concerned about a future in which he might not be in a position to ensure that his child received the very best of care.

'Maybe I'm thinking that after what you did to me you might be a bad influence to have in a child's life,' Zara told him honestly.

In receipt of that admission, his strong bone structure showed prominently below his bronzed skin and his jaw line clenched hard. In one sense he was outraged that Monty Blake's daughter could question his integrity when her father had none whatsoever. But he could hardly expect her to appreciate that when he had deceived her in Tuscany. He should be grateful, however, that she refused to see him as her only support in a hostile world just because she had fallen pregnant by him. After all, just how much was he prepared to sacrifice to ensure his child's welfare?

'I'm trying to forge a new and different relationship with you,' he delivered tautly.

She gazed into his stunning dark eyes and it was as if a thousand butterflies fluttered free in the pit of her stomach. Instantly she closed him out again, refusing to be entrapped by his raw physical appeal. 'I can't give you a fresh start with me. I don't forgive men who try to use me.'

His brows drew together as he picked up on the pained note she could not suppress. 'There was someone else? Who? What did he do?'

Zara dealt him a bleak look and then wondered what she had to hide. Maybe if she explained he'd understand that there was no way back into her good graces. 'I met Julian when I was eighteen. He was twenty five and he told me he loved me. After he had asked me to marry him he took me away for a weekend. The first night he got me drunk in our hotel room…' Her strained voice ran out of steam and power, her heart-shaped face drawn, her eyes haunted by unpleasant memories. 'I must've passed out. When I came round he had me handcuffed half naked to the headboard of the bed—'

'He had you…*what*?' Vitale repeated in thunderous disbelief.

'When I opened my eyes he had a camera trained on me. All he wanted was sleazy photos of me undressed, so that he could blackmail my father with them. He took my clothes off while I was unconscious. He hadn't even bothered to wait until after he had slept with me—but then he wasn't that interested.' A laugh that had a wounded edge fell from her lips. 'In fact he said I wasn't really his type, he preferred curvy brunettes—'

'Per amor di Dio!' Vitale had a disturbing image of her naked and bewildered, innocent and frightened. The newly protective instincts he had formed since he learnt of her pregnancy were inflamed by the idea of her being stripped of her dignity and at the mercy of a man who only saw her as a source of profit. Julian had badly betrayed her trust when she was still very young and naïve. Vitale refused to think about the damage he might have done pursuing revenge on his sister's account. Regretting the past was always, in his opinion, a waste of time.

'My father may be a womaniser but he's a complete dinosaur when it comes to the behaviour of the women in his family and very conscious of his public image. He paid up and the photos were destroyed although I still haven't heard the last of that disaster even now,' Zara confided painfully. 'I got Julian thrown in my face again last week and the week before. I was young and stupid and too easily impressed, but that's twice I've seriously embarrassed my family now.'

'But what Julian did was criminal. He assaulted you. You father should've reported him to the police.'

'Dad didn't want to risk the newspapers getting hold of the story. It's ancient history now.' Zara's tone was dismissive and she lifted her chin. 'And I thought I had learned my lesson with Julian, but then I met you.'

'What happened between us in Italy is over and done with—'

'Is it? It may be over but it's not forgotten,' Zara pointed out, her quiet voice harshening with the antipathy she was struggling to restrain. 'And I'm not going to give you the chance to cause me any more grief.'

Vitale realised that in the light she saw him now, only the ultimate sacrifice was likely to convince her of the strength of his intentions. With every fibre of his being he baulked at that option, for marriage was a hell of a price to pay for a contraceptive oversight. Yet how else could he make sure that he had a permanent place in his future child's life? How else could he acquire the legal rights with which he could always protect his child from any threat? And how could she possibly cope well as a single parent without adequate family support? Yet if he married her, he would lose the freedom he valued, the choices he luxuriated in and the privacy he had always cherished. Suppressing his reluctance and his resentment, Vitale recalled his own wretched childhood and accepted that no price was too high if it protected his unborn son or daughter from the risk of growing up in a similar hell.

Vitale studied Zara carefully. 'Will that answer still hold good even if I ask you to marry me?'

Zara jerked in astonishment, her brow furrowing, her eyes wide as she decided that that must be his idea of a joke after what she had told him about Julian using a marriage proposal to gain her trust. 'You can't be serious.'

'I am perfectly serious—I'm asking you to be my

wife,' Vitale countered with cool assurance. 'In the hope that we can raise our child together.'

'Not so long ago you told me that you avoided women with wedding rings in their eyes and that that's why you're still single,' she reminded him ruefully.

'But then you fell pregnant with my child and naturally my priorities altered,' Vitale pointed out drily. 'We can't turn the clock back. We have to look to the future.'

Her appetite having disappeared in tune with the tension rising in the atmosphere, Zara pushed aside the dessert and stood up, her eyes dark with strain. If an offer of marriage was his attempt at restitution he could forget it—she was not about to be taken in again. 'No, absolutely not. You don't need to worry. The baby and I will be fine on our own. Thankfully I'm not a helpless teenage girl with no idea how to manage—'

Vitale was not convinced by that argument. He sprang up to his full commanding height, the vital force and energy of his gaze welded to her. 'We have to talk this out. Don't leave.'

Zara veiled her eyes and fought to recapture the composure he had cracked with his astonishing proposal. 'I wasn't leaving yet. I've brought the villa plan with me. If you've finished eating we can look at it now.'

Desperate for a distraction, Zara removed the plan from the tube and spread it on the unused portion of the polished table. She explained the meaning of various symbols she had used and discussed possibilities. Vitale was impressed by the intricate detail of the design, not having appreciated that she would actually be drawing the plans with her own fair hand.

'Those borders—could some of them be left empty?'

Her brow furrowed. 'Yes, of course, but—'

'The lady whom I hope will be living there,' Vitale began with uncharacteristic hesitancy lacing his dark deep voice, 'may have an interest in the garden and if the planting is not quite complete that may encourage her to get more involved.'

'That's a good idea,' Zara remarked, insanely curious about the identity of the individual, for he had been careful to keep that information confidential when they had been together in Italy. His innate reserve would always seek to impose distance between them, she registered. He was not a man given to casual confidences and he kept his own counsel. Working out what made him tick would always be a challenge for her.

Zara laughed when Fluffy nudged her ankle with one of her toys and Vitale watched in surprise as Zara threw it and the rabbit played fetch. 'She loves games,' she told him, a natural smile chasing the tension from her lush mouth.

Vitale watched her stroke the rabbit's head with delicate fingers. She was so gentle with the little animal and it clearly adored her. 'I was serious about the proposal,' he asserted, exasperated that she could think otherwise.

'Being pregnant isn't a good enough reason to get married,' Zara replied doggedly, her senses awakened by the faint aromatic hint of his cologne assailing her nostrils because he was standing close to her. Even the scent of him was awesomely familiar. Her spine stiffened as tingling warmth pooled at the heart of her, her body instantly reacting to the proximity of his. He was pure temptation but she was too much on her guard to betray the weakness he could evoke.

His frustration increasing, Vitale stared down at her with brooding dark eyes. 'It is very important to me that I should be in a position to play a proper part in my child's life—'

'You don't have to marry me to play that part—'

Thinking of his destroyed childhood with his cruel stepfather, Vitale barely repressed a shudder of disagreement. 'If we're not married, if we stay separate, we will both end up with other partners and it will be much more difficult—'

'But other people manage it,' Zara sliced in flatly even as her heart clenched at the very thought of him with another woman.

It was going to happen, possibly had even happened already, she scolded herself angrily. Vitale was going to be with other women and she had to adapt to that idea. That the idea bothered her was just some weird jealous and possessive prompting, most probably because he had become her first lover. On the other hand, a scheming little voice murmured somewhere in the depths of her brain, if *you* married him, nobody else could have him. She stifled that inner voice, embarrassed by its foolishness.

The following morning Zara attended an appointment with her GP. He confirmed the test results and sent her off to see the practice nurse, who gave her a bunch of leaflets packed with pregnancy advice. They were still clutched in her hand when a man walking past her in the street knocked her shoulder, loosening her grip so that the sheets spun across the pavement in an arc. As the man sped on without noticing Zara stooped to pick up the leaflets.

'Zara?' a familiar voice queried and Zara straightened, recognising the elegant brunette. 'I wasn't expecting to see you round this neighbourhood. Didn't I hear that you'd moved to another part of town?'

Meeting Ella's big blue curious eyes, Zara reddened. 'Yes, I have—'

'Oh, my goodness, are those for you?' Ella exclaimed, flicking one of the leaflets, which clearly showed a pregnant woman, with a manicured fingernail and accompanying the question with a delighted squeal. 'Are you pregnant?'

'I'm meeting someone in ten minutes. Lovely seeing you again, Ella,' Zara fielded with a bright smile, stuffing the informative leaflets into her bag and walking on without further comment. Her cheeks were hot as she queried her bad luck at running into one of the biggest gossips she knew at the wrong moment.

Vitale was not having a good day either. He had offered to fall on his sword like a proper little soldier when he had asked her to marry him. The sacrifice had been necessary: she was carrying his baby and he had a deep need to be a genuine part of his child's life. But it would also entail sharing his life. When had he ever dreamt of sharing his life with another person?

When had he ever longed for a child of his own? He had never wanted those things and his entire life had been devoted to achieving emotional self-sufficiency. He told himself that he should be grateful that she had turned him down. He should walk away while he could, avoid getting personally involved. He should be content to ensure that his only responsibility towards her and the child was financial. Why could he not settle for that eminently practical option? Realistically what were the chances that Zara would some day bring a man into her life as brutal as Vitale's late stepfather?

Zara was at Blooming Perfect going through the accounts with Rob when Jono phoned her and drew her attention to a paragraph in a gossip column. Although she was grateful for the warning her heart sank and she went out to buy the paper and there it was, clearly the result of a tip-off from Ella or one of her pals, the loaded suggestion that party girl and socialite Zara Blake might be expecting a baby. Her phone rang again: it was her mother asking her to come home for a chat.

Zara knew what she was going to be asked and she definitely didn't want to go and face the music. Unfortunately being adult and independent demanded that she not avoid the inevitable, no matter how unpleasant it might prove to be. Monty and Ingrid Blake were going to be even more disappointed in her than they already were. An unmarried pregnant daughter was no consolation for one who mere weeks ago had been set to marry a Greek billionaire in the society wedding of the year.

'Is it true?' Ingrid Blake demanded the instant her daughter entered the sparsely furnished drawing room where elegance counted for more than comfort.

Her heart beating very fast, Zara glanced nervously at her father standing by the fireplace, his still-handsome face set hard as granite. 'Yes, I'm pregnant.'

'We'll organise a termination for you straight away,' her mother said without an ounce of hesitation.

Zara straightened her slight shoulders and eased them back. 'No. I want to have my baby.'

'Who's the father?' Monty Blake growled.

'I'm sorry but I don't want to discuss that.'

'I bet you don't, you brainless little—' the older man launched furiously at her, a red flush of rage staining his cheeks.

Her tension palpable, Zara's mother rested a soothing hand lightly on her husband's arm. 'Don't let her upset you, darling… She's not worth it—'

'You're telling me, she's not!' Monty Blake seethed, grinding his teeth as he strode forward, his face a mask of fury. 'It's out of the question for you to have this baby.'

Struggling not to back away from her enraged parent as she had so often seen her mother do without any happy result, Zara stood her ground.

'Listen to your father for once, Zara,' Ingrid ordered thinly. 'You simply *can't* have this baby! Be reasonable. Once you have a child in tow, your life will be ruined.'

'Did Tom and I ruin your life?' Zara asked painfully, deeply hurt that her mother could so immediately dismiss the prospect of her first grandchild being born.

'Don't you dare mention your brother's name, you stupid little cow!' Monty Blake spat at her, erupting into a white hot rage at that fatal reference and swinging up his hand to slap her hard across one cheekbone.

Eyes filling with fear and pain, Zara was almost unbalanced by the force of that blow and she had to step back to stay upright. Her hand crept up to press against her hot, stinging cheek. 'Don't you dare hit me,' she told her father angrily. 'I should call the police on you—'

'Don't be silly,' her mother interrupted in alarm at such a threat from her daughter. 'You asked for it.'

'The same way you always did?' Zara prompted shakily before turning scornful eyes on her father. 'I'll never set foot in this house again.'

'We'll live,' her father shot back at her with derision. 'You're no loss!'

Sick with shock in the aftermath of that traumatic confrontation, Zara returned to her apartment. When she climbed out of her car she could feel something trickling down her face and when she dashed it away saw blood on the side of her hand. In her compact mirror she saw the cut on her cheek where the stone in her father's signet ring must have broken the skin. She couldn't still the shaking in her body, but she was asking herself why she was so surprised by what had happened for, although it was the first time that her father had hit her since she had become an adult, it was far from being the first time that he had struck her.

It was a fact of Zara's childhood that Monty Blake had an unmanageable temper and that he lashed out with his fists whenever he lost control. Usually Ingrid had paid the price of her husband's need for violence to satisfy his rage or frustration. In fact as a terrified child of ten years old seeing her mother beaten up Zara had once called the police and the fallout from that unwelcome intervention had taught her an unforgettable lesson. Branded a wicked liar and winning even her twin's censure for 'letting down' the family, she had been sent away to boarding school. That night she had learned that anything that happened behind the doors of the Blakes' smart town house was strictly private and not for sharing, not even with Bee.

'It's between Mum and Dad—it's nothing to do with us. He hardly ever lifts the hand to either of us,' Tom used to point out when they were teenagers. 'It's only the odd slap or punch—I'm sure there's a lot worse goes on in other families.'

But dread of their father's sudden violent outbursts had created a horribly intimidating atmosphere in Zara's home while she was growing up. All of them had worked very hard at trying to please or soothe Monty Blake. Tom, the apple of his father's eye, had always been the most successful. The aggressive attacks on their mother, however, had continued in secret for occasionally Zara had noticed that her mother was moving slowly and stiffly as if she was in pain and had known that her father was usually too careful to plant a fist where a bruise might show.

By the time she reached her apartment stress had given Zara a nasty headache and her face was hurting her like mad. She was on the brink of taking painkillers before she remembered that she was pregnant and realised that without medical advice it would be safer to do without medication. She examined her swollen cheekbone in the mirror. It was hot and red and a livid scratch trailed across her skin while the darkening of her eye socket suggested that a bruise was forming. When the buzzer on her door sounded she snatched up her sunglasses and put them on.

It was Vitale, long and lean in a black business suit and impatiently about to stab on the buzzer a second time when she opened the door. His hand fell back from the wood and he stared down at her.

'Why are you wearing sunglasses indoors?' he questioned, strolling past her although she had not invited him in.

Just as Zara frowned Vitale flipped the specs off her nose and stilled when he saw her battered face. 'What the hell happened to you?' he growled angrily.

'I fell…tripped at the nursery,' she lied.

'Don't lie to me. I can spot a lie at sixty paces,' Vitale warned her, frowning as he traced the swelling with a gentle fingertip. 'This looks more like someone punched you.'

'Don't be ridiculous,' Zara said in a wobbly voice, her eyes welling up with tears. 'Why are you here?'

Vitale tossed down the newspaper he carried in a silent statement. It was the same edition that had implied that she might be pregnant.

'Oh, that…' she muttered abstractedly as he closed the door behind him. Although she had only read that gossip column this morning it already felt as if a hundred years had passed since then.

'I don't believe that you fell. I want to know who did that to your face. Who hit you?' Vitale breathed soft and low, but there was a fire in his penetrating gaze. 'I think you might have a black eye tomorrow.'

Nervousness made it difficult for Zara to swallow and her throat was tight. She was tired and upset and sore. 'It's not important.'

'You've been assaulted. How can that not be important?' Vitale demanded, cutting through her weary voice. 'Who are you trying to protect?'

Zara paled at that accurate stab in the dark, but the habit of secrecy where her family was concerned was too deeply engrained in her to be easily broken. 'I'm not protecting anyone.'

'You're pregnant. What sort of a person attacks a pregnant woman?' he demanded rawly. 'He could have hit your stomach rather than your face, causing you to miscarry—would you still be protecting him then?'

The hunted expression in Zara's strained eyes deepened as she dropped her head to avoid his searing gaze. 'I don't want to talk about this, Vitale.'

He closed a hand round hers and drew her closer. 'I'm not leaving until you tell me. When you were attacked our child was put at risk and I can't walk away from that.'

Reminded of her responsibility towards the baby she carried, Zara was engulfed by a dreadful tide of guilt. Her opposing loyalties made her feel torn in two and suddenly her resistance washed away in the tide of her distress. 'It was my father...okay?' she cried defiantly as she wrenched her hand free of Vitale's hold. 'But he didn't mean anything by it—he just loses his temper and lashes out—'

'Your...*father*?' His eyes flaring like golden fireworks, Vitale's angry voice actually shook, his accent thickening around the syllables as he yanked open the door again.

'Where are you going?' In consternation, Zara followed him and grabbed his arm to force him to stop in his tracks. 'What do you think you're going to do?'

Eyes veiled, Vitale rested his livid gaze on her anxious face. 'I'll make sure that this never happens again.'

'How can you do that? I don't want you fighting with my father... I don't want people to find out about this—it's private!' Zara gasped, clutching at the well-cut jacket of his business suit with frantic hands.

Vitale closed his fingers round her fragile wrists and gently detached her grip. His face was forbidding in its austerity, his eyes hard as iron. 'I'm not about to fight with your father. I am not planning to tell anyone else about this either—that is your choice to make. But I *am* going to make sure that he never ever dares to lay a finger on you again,' he spelt out in a wrathful undertone. 'I'll see you later.'

Left alone, Zara trembled from the force of all the emotions she was fighting to contain. She was shaking with stress. Her father would lose his head again when Vitale approached him and made his accusation. The older man would know that once again his daughter had talked. A headache hammered painfully behind her taut brow and she sank down on the edge of the bed and breathed in slow and deep in an attempt to calm down. She was appalled by Vitale's interference but even more shocked that she had surrendered and told him the truth. For so many years she had kept that family shame a deep, dark secret. Now all hell was about to break loose because she had just given a man who already hated her father another reason to despise and attack him.

For an instant though Zara was mentally swept back to the elegant drawing room where she had been rocked back on her heels by her father's blow. Whether she liked it or not she had to admit that Vitale had made a valid point. Had she fallen she might have injured her baby or even miscarried. There was no excuse for her father's violence; there never had been an excuse for his behaviour. But while she accepted that truth, intellectually dealing with something that had become so much a part of her family life was altogether something else. It had been her mother's refusal to condemn her husband's violence that had set the agenda of acceptance in Zara's home. Although it hurt to admit it, her brother Tom's insistence on ignoring the problem had also given strength to the idea that such violence had to be endured and concealed. Of course, her father had never struck Tom. Monty Blake had always aimed his violence at his womenfolk.

Feeling too sick to eat, Zara lay down on the bed and eventually fell asleep. Vitale's return wakened her and she answered the door barefoot, her hair a tousled silvery cloud round her face as she blinked up at him drowsily. She was startled to see her father standing by

Vitale's side. In the shadow of Vitale's greater height and raw energy, Monty Blake looked pale, wretched and diminished.

'Your father has something he wants to say to you,' Vitale proclaimed harshly.

'I'm sorry I hurt you—it will never happen again,' her father muttered with all the life of a battery-operated robot.

'I'm not having a termination,' she reiterated in a feverish whisper, wanting her father to know that that was not a price she was prepared to pay for family forgiveness.

In response to that revealing statement a murderous light flamed in Vitale's gaze. 'We're getting married as soon as it can be arranged,' he delivered.

Taken aback by the announcement, Zara shot him a confused glance. After all, he was already well aware of her thoughts on that subject. Dark eyes gleaming with purpose, Vitale stared back at her in blatant challenge. She parted her lips to argue and then decided to wait until her father was no longer present. She felt she owed Vitale that much after he had brought her father to her door to apologise to her. For the first time ever a man had tried to protect Zara rather than take advantage of her and she could only be impressed by that reality.

'You must do as you see fit,' Monty Blake responded flatly, turning back to Vitale to add, 'Are you satisfied?'

'For the moment, but watch your step around me and your daughter.'

Zara watched her father hurry back into the lift, keen to make his escape, and she slowly breathed in and out, the worst of her tension evaporating with his departure. 'How on earth did you persuade him to come here?'

'I didn't persuade him, I threatened him,' Vitale admitted without an ounce of regret. 'He's terrified of being forced to face the legal and social consequences of his behaviour. I'm surprised that you've never used that fear against him.'

Zara lowered her lashes, thinking of how she had been branded a troublemaking liar at the age of ten when she had tried to report her father's violence to the authorities. Nobody had backed up her story, not even her mother, and by the end of it all nobody had believed her either.

'He's hit you before, hasn't he?' Vitale prompted darkly.

'This was the first time since I grew up,' Zara admitted grudgingly. 'I don't think he can help himself. I think he needs professional help or anger-management classes but he wouldn't go to anything like that. He won't admit he has a problem.'

'Does he hit your mother?'

Zara glanced at his lean strong face and then looked away from the condemnation etched there to nod jerkily in reluctant confirmation. 'She won't do anything about it, won't even talk about it. I'm glad you didn't hit him though.'

'I would have enjoyed smashing his teeth down his throat,' Vitale admitted with a casual ease that shook her. 'But it wouldn't have helped anyone. Domestic violence is like an addiction for some men, but I believe that in your father's case the threat of public exposure might have forced him to seek treatment.'

'Did you confront him about your sister? About what happened the night that she drowned?' Zara pressed in a strained undertone.

There was a bitter light in his eyes and his sardonic mouth twisted. 'No, it wasn't the right moment for me to demand those answers. I was more concerned about you.'

Vitale swung away, his last words still echoing inside his head; even he questioned his own restraint. How could he have been more concerned about her? Granted she carried his child, but he had spent half a lifetime dreaming of a confrontation with Monty Blake. Only to discover that, in the flesh, Monty Blake was scarcely a challenging target. Loredana's former lover was a weak man, easily cowed by a more forceful personality and the threat of social humiliation.

Zara was frowning as well, marvelling that Vitale had had her father at such a disadvantage and yet had remained silent in spite of his fierce desire for revenge. 'Did he realise who you were? Didn't he recognise your name from your sister's?'

'Loredana and I had different surnames. Her name was Barigo.' His lean strong face had taken on a shuttered aspect that warned her she had touched on a sensitive subject. Vitale, she realised belatedly, had family secrets as well.

'Why on earth did you tell him that we were getting married?'

Vitale threw back his handsome dark head and settled his moody gaze on her. 'I'm convinced that when you consider your options you'll see that you have nothing to lose and everything to gain by becoming my wife—'

'How?' Zara interrupted baldly. 'I've already told you how I feel about you.'

'Take a risk on me.'

Her lips compressed. 'I don't take risks—'

'But I do. That's why I'm the CEO of a major investment bank,' Vitale told her with savage assurance. 'It makes sense for you to give marriage a chance for our child's sake. If it doesn't work out, we can get a divorce. But at least we'll know that we tried.'

Taken aback by his speech, Zara was momentarily silenced. *For our child's sake,* four little words that had immense impact on her impression of Vitale Roccanti, much as his earlier defence of her against her father had had. Slowly but surely Vitale was changing her opinion of him. Her father might not have added anything positive to her life but Vitale, she sensed, would be a far different prospect in the parenting stakes. Vitale was willing to put his money where his mouth was and put their baby's needs to the top of the pile. He was a handsome, wealthy and successful man yet he was still willing to give up his freedom to provide a more stable background for the child he had accidentally fathered. She could only admire him for that and admit that, given the choice, she would much prefer to raise her child with two parents.

'If we get married and it falls apart, it would be very upsetting for everyone concerned.'

'I would find watching you raise my child with another man infinitely *more* upsetting,' Vitale countered with blunt emphasis. 'All I'm asking you to do is give us the opportunity to see if we can make it work.'

'It's not that simple—'

Vitale released his breath in a driven hiss of impatience. 'You're the one making it complicated.'

Zara's tiny frame was rigid. Could she take a risk and give him another chance? But marriage wasn't an experiment. She could not marry him on a casual basis and walk away without concern if it failed. In her experience failure always bit deep and hurt. And just how far could she trust a man she couldn't read with any accuracy? 'I don't know enough about you. I can't forget that you plotted and planned against me.'

'I can put that past behind us if I have to, *angelina mia*. Our child's needs take precedence,' Vitale contended.

The silence buzzed. Her troubled gaze lingering on his wide, sensual mouth, she recalled the taste of him with a hot liquid surge low in her tummy that she struggled to quell. The tender flesh between her thighs dampened and a pink flush of awareness covered her face. Tensing, she looked hurriedly away from him.

'But I will be honest—I also want you,' Vitale conceded in a dark driven undertone, startling her with that additional admission. 'That's not what I chose, not what I foresaw and certainly not what I'm comfortable with. But it *is* how I feel right now. Ever since we were together in Italy I've wanted you back in my bed again.'

Although she flushed, Zara stood a little straighter,

strengthened by that raw-edged confession. It did her good to know that he was not quite as in control as he liked to pretend. Every time she looked at him she had to fight her natural response to his sleek dark magnetism. The idea that he had to fight the same attraction had considerable appeal. He bent his arrogant head, eyes narrowed to track her every change of expression with a lethal sensuality as integral to him as his aggressive take on life.

'All right, I'll give marrying you a trial for three months,' Zara declared, tilting her chin. 'If we can't make it work in that time we have to agree to split up without any recriminations on either side.'

'A sort of "try before you buy" option?' Vitale drawled silkily.

'Why not?' Feeling as though she was somewhat in control of events again, Zara settled her soft full lips into a wary smile. She could handle being attracted to him as long as he was attracted to her. If she kept a sensible grip on her emotions there was no reason why she should get hurt. Furthermore, after what he had done to her she would never make the mistake of viewing him through rose-coloured glasses again.

His hand curving to her narrow shoulder, Vitale lowered his head and claimed her mouth with his. As he pried her lips apart with the tip of his tongue an arrow of sizzling heat slivered through her with such piercing, drugging sweetness that she shivered violently in response. She dug her nails into her palms to stop herself from reaching out to him and she stood there stiff as a board while the greedy warmth and excitement of desire washed through her every skin cell, filling her with restless energy and longing.

He lifted his head again, dark golden eyes blazing with unconcealed hunger. 'I'll *make* it work for us,' he swore.

But the very fact that he acknowledged a need to work at their marriage was, to her way of thinking, the most likely reason why their efforts would fail. Natural inclinations often outgunned the best of good intentions, she reflected worriedly. Only when the going got tough would they discover how deep their commitment to a practical marriage could actually go.

CHAPTER EIGHT

Two weeks before the wedding, Vitale arranged to pick Zara up for lunch. Not having seen him at all in the preceding week owing to his demanding schedule, she was surprised by the invitation.

'I thought you were always too busy during the day for this sort of thing,' Zara reminded him of his own words on the phone several nights earlier as she climbed into his car.

'As a rule I am but this is rather different. We're going to see your father,' Vitale revealed grimly.

Her head swivelled, eyes bright with dismay and curiosity in her disconcerted face. 'Why the hell are we meeting up with Dad?'

'It's time I asked those questions about my sister's death,' Vitale volunteered tight-mouthed, his brooding tension palpable in the taut lines of his face. 'Now that we are getting married those questions have to finally be answered. He's your father. I can't leave you out of this.'

'I'm not sure I want to be there,' she confessed, disturbed by the prospect of being on the sidelines of such a sensitive confrontation. 'Although it hardly matters as relations currently stand between me and my parents, Dad won't forgive me for being present if you're planning to humiliate him.'

'I see no advantage to doing that,' Vitale admitted flatly fingers flexing and tightening round the steering wheel. 'I phoned your father first thing this morning and told him that I was Loredana's brother and that I need him to tell me the truth of what happened the night she drowned. He's had a few hours to think over his options.'

'And you think an upfront approach will work like some kind of magic charm with him?' Zara pressed doubtfully.

'Your father is not a stupid man. What does he have to lose? He knows I probably can't disprove anything he says. There were only two crew members on board that yacht. The stewardess, who was also the cook, died. Rod Baines, the sailor in charge of the boat, suffered head injuries and remembered very little about that night after he had recovered.'

Monty Blake was in his office on the first floor of the elegant flagship hotel of the Royale chain. He was standing by the window when they entered and he swung round, his mouth tightening with annoyance when he saw his daughter. 'Did you know about this connection when you got involved with the man you're planning to marry?' he demanded accusingly.

'That's not relevant. Why don't you just tell Vitale what happened that night?' Zara replied evenly.

'I told the full story at the inquest many years ago—'

'Yes, I believe you magically found yourself in the rescue dinghy and then fell conveniently unconscious while the yacht sank,' Vitale breathed witheringly. 'How long were you a part of my sister's life before that night?'

The older man grimaced. 'I wasn't a part of her life. I hardly knew her—'

'But she was pregnant—'

'Not by me, as I stated at the inquest,' Zara's father insisted quick as a flash. 'I was never intimate with her.'

Vitale frowned. 'Do I look like a fool?'

'I never got the chance. Check out the dates if you don't believe me. I met Loredana at your uncle's country house, dined with her the following week while I was at our hotel in Rome and invited her to go sailing with me at the weekend. She was a very beautiful young woman but it was a casual thing,' he declared, shooting a look of discomfiture at his daughter. 'I had quite enough complications in my life. Your mother and I were hardly speaking to each other at the time.'

Zara stiffened. 'Nothing you tell us will go beyond these walls,' she promised uneasily.

'Loredana was in a very emotional mood when she joined me that weekend,' Monty Blake revealed. 'Over our meal she admitted that she'd had a row with some boyfriend and that she was pregnant. It was hardly what I had signed up for when I invited her onto the yacht for a pleasure trip and we had a difference of opinion when I asked her why she had agreed to join me on board—'

'An argument?' Vitale queried darkly, his suspicions obvious.

'There was no big drama,' the older man replied wearily. 'Apparently Loredana only accepted my invite because she wanted to make her boyfriend jealous. She hoped he would try to stop her seeing me but he didn't and she was upset about that. When she started crying I suggested she retire to her cabin for the night—and I mean no disrespect when I say that I'd had quite enough of her histrionics by then.'

Vitale managed not to flinch but he did remember his sister as being a very emotional and vivid individual, easily roused to laughter, temper or tears. There had been no reference to an argument, no mention of Loredana's supposedly troubled state of mind during the inquest. But for all that there was a convincing ring of authenticity to the older man's story and he could imagine how irritated Monty Blake must have been when he realised why Loredana had accepted his invitation and that his seduction plans were unlikely to come to anything.

'Your sister made me feel like I was too old to be chasing girls her age,' Zara's father claimed with a curled lip. 'She depressed me. I didn't go to bed. I sat up getting very drunk that night and fell asleep in the saloon. Some time during the night, Rod, the chap in charge of the boat, woke me up, said there was a bad storm. He told me to go and fetch your sister and Pam, the stewardess, while he sorted the escape dinghy. He said the two women were together…' Monty shook his greying head heavily. 'I was drunk and the generator failed, so the lights went out…'

'And then what did you do?' Vitale growled.

'Your sister wasn't in her cabin and I didn't know my way round the crew quarters. The yacht was lurching in every direction. I couldn't see where I was going or keep my feet. I started shouting their names. Water was streaming down the gangway. It was terrifying. I fell and hurt myself. I rushed back up on deck to get Rod to help but Rod had been injured and he was bleeding heavily from a head wound.' Something of the desperation Monty Blake had felt that night had leaked into his fracturing voice and stamped his drawn face with the recollection of a nightmare. 'The boat was sinking and I panicked. Is that what you want me to admit?'

'All I want is the truth,' Vitale breathed tightly, almost as strained as Zara's father.

'Well, I'm sorry I wasn't a hero, but with the sea pouring in I was too scared to go below deck alone again,' he gritted in a shamed but also defiant undertone, as if that was a moment and a decision he had weighed many times over the years that had passed since that fateful night. 'I pulled on a life jacket and helped Rod into his, struggled with the dinghy while he tried to tell me what to do. I can't swim, you know…I never learned. The boat was going down, there was no time for a search, no time to do anything else—'

'You hardly knew her,' Vitale remarked with hollow finality. 'You saved yourself. I don't believe it would be fair to judge you for that. '

Zara never did get lunch. They left the hotel in silence. Neither of them had any appetite after that meeting. She knew Vitale's thoughts were still on his dead sister. She knew the truth had been hard for him to hear. Loredana had been very young and agreeing to go sailing with a virtual stranger had clearly been an impulsive act. Her father had been drunk and less than brave in an emergency, but only a special few were willing to risk their own life for another person's and it wouldn't be fair to blame him for falling short of a heroic ideal.

'No, there's not even a hint of a little bump!' Bee declared two weeks later on Zara's wedding day, as she scrutinised her half-sister's stomach from every angle. Bee reckoned that only a woman who had never had a weight problem would have fallen pregnant and then chosen a figure-hugging wedding gown calculated to reveal the smallest bulge. Luckily for Zara, she had no surplus flesh to spoil the perfect symmetry of her flowing lace dress.

Zara studied her reflection, grateful that her pregnancy did not yet show. True, her breasts were a little fuller, but that was the sole change in her shape that she had noticed. Her gown was slender and elegant, maximising her diminutive height. 'I hope Vitale doesn't think I'm overdressed.'

'How can you be overdressed at your own wedding?' Bee demanded.

'When it's a quiet do with only a couple of witnesses attending,' Zara pointed out, wincing at that reality.

'Does that bother you?' Bee asked worriedly. 'I know

this can't be the sort of wedding you ever expected to have.'

'It's what I want. I was never into all the fuss and frills of the wedding arrangements Mum insisted on when I was supposed to be marrying Sergios,' Zara admitted, a look of discomfiture crossing her delicate features, 'and this wedding is still only a formality—'

'I think it's a little more than a formality when the man you're about to marry is the father of your baby,' Bee cut in with some amusement.

'I'm very grateful that Vitale's willing to share that responsibility.'

Bee pulled an unimpressed face. 'Which is exactly why you picked a gorgeous dress and got all dollied up in your fanciest make-up and shoes for Vitale's benefit?' she teased. '*Please*, do I look that stupid?'

Zara said nothing, for it was true that she had gone to no end of trouble to look her very best for the occasion. She had not required a church full of guests as an excuse to push the glamour boat out. But it had taken an ironic ton of make-up and every scrap of artistry she possessed to achieve the natural effect she had sought. The natural effect she knew he admired. Her shoes, sparkling with diamanté, were the very cute equivalent of Cinderella's slippers. To satisfy the something-old rhyme she had her late brother's school badge tucked into her bra and her thigh sported a blue garter. If the wedding was only a formality why had she bothered with all those trappings?

The circumstances being what they were, she had only invited her half-sisters to share the brief ceremony with her. Bee was accompanying her to the church and Tawny had promised to meet them there. Afterwards she and Vitale were flying straight out to Italy. She had packed up her apartment, surrendered it and had spent the previous night with Bee. She was retaining Rob to manage Blooming Perfect in London. She was hoping that there would be sufficient demand for her services in Tuscany for her to open another small branch of the business. Fluffy had already flown out to her future new home. Zara, however, was as apprehensive as a climber hanging onto a frayed rope: she was terrified that she was doing the wrong thing. In one life there was only room for so many mistakes and on this occasion she was very conscious that she had a child's welfare to consider.

The car Vitale had sent to collect her drew up outside the church. She got out with Bee's assistance and her younger sister, Tawny, hurried towards her.

'Zara!' she exclaimed, pushing a long curl of fiery copper hair out of her eyes. 'You look amazing! Who is this Italian? And why didn't I get the chance to meet him before this?'

'I'm pregnant and we're in a hurry,' Zara confided, watching her sibling's bright blue eyes shoot wide in surprise and drop almost inevitably to her stomach.

'Oh…' Tawny grimaced. 'And you're marrying him? I hope you know what you're doing—'

'When does Zara ever know what she's doing?' Bee chimed in ruefully. 'She never takes the long view.'

'My sisters are supposed to be universally supportive on my wedding day,' Zara cut in with a warning frown. 'Get supporting.'

And nothing more was said. Her siblings escorted her up the church steps and smoothed out the hem of her gown in the porch. The organ began to play and the doors opened for Zara to walk down the aisle. Marriage, she was thinking on the edge of panic, marriage was such a big complex step. Was she even cut out to be a wife? There was so much she didn't know about Vitale, so much they hadn't discussed. He was waiting at the altar, his head held high, and she needn't have worried about being overdressed because he and the man by his side were kitted out in fancy grey morning suits.

At the exact moment that Vitale turned his handsome head to look at her, his gaze every bit as edgy as her own, her apprehension evaporated because he smiled. A wolfish smile that took him from being a very good-looking guy to an absolutely gorgeous one. There was admiration in his gaze and she basked in it.

'*Like* the dress,' he breathed in a discreet aside before the vicar began to speak. 'You look wonderful.'

The last knot of tension in her stomach dissolved into a feeling of warmth and acceptance. The ceremony progressed and her hand stayed steady as he slid a wedding ring on her finger. And then almost dizzyingly fast the service was over, the organ music was swelling and Vitale was escorting her back down the aisle, a light hand resting on hers. In the porch he met her siblings and she learned that his companion was his lawyer and also a friend from his university days.

They drove straight to the airport.

'Did you mind that your parents weren't part of the ceremony?' Vitale asked her as soon as they were alone.

'Not at all. It wouldn't have been fancy enough for my mother and somehow my father would have found a way of ruining the day by calling me stupid.' Her soft mouth compressed and she shrugged a forlorn shoulder, conscious of his bewildered appraisal and saying nothing more.

'Why would he have done that?'

'I should have told you by now—I suffer from dyslexia. *Badly*,' Zara stressed, her hands tightly curled together on her lap because it took courage to confess a weakness that had been regarded with such disgust by her family. 'Regardless of what my father thinks, though, I'm not slow-witted. I have some difficulty reading, writing and spelling but I manage most things fine with the help of a computer.'

Vitale frowned because he was recalling her blank appraisal of the instructions on the pregnancy test and suddenly he was rethinking that scene with a tight feeling inside his chest. The anxiety, the fear of rejection, in her gaze screamed at him. He realised that, regardless of her attempt to refer casually to the condition, what she had just admitted was a very big deal for her. 'I went to school with a couple of dyslexics. I know you're not slow-witted and fortunately dyslexics can get a lot of help these days.'

Zara grimaced. 'My father doesn't believe dyslexia exists. He just thinks I'm stupid and he wouldn't allow me to have speech-language therapy.'

'That's ridiculous. Didn't you get help at school?'

'I was sixteen before I was diagnosed and I left a few months later. Although I dropped out of my A-level studies, I do manage,' she said again, clearly keen to drop the subject.

He remembered how pale and tense she had been while she struggled with those instructions, clearly terrified of him realising that she had a problem, and his rage with Monty Blake roared up through him like volcanic lava. Instead of being taught how to cope with the disorder, she had been taught to be ashamed of it and left to struggle alone. He wondered why that image bothered him, why he should feel so angry on her behalf. When had he ever felt protective about a woman? Only once before and even then his intelligence warning him to keep his distance had warred with more natural instincts.

'It's never too late to learn. Some sessions with a professional would help you handle the condition now,' Vitale remarked evenly. 'And lift your confidence.'

Zara went pink. She bit back the tart comment that she was sure he hadn't expected to take a wife still in need of lessons, because she was well aware that when she put herself down she was revealing low self-esteem. Furthermore she recognised that he had seen shrewdly right to the heart of her problem. Her family's attitude to her dyslexia had imposed secrecy on her and her subsequent fear of exposure had only made the problem worse.

'I thought you'd be embarrassed that I'm a dyslexic.'

'It would take a great deal more to embarrass me, *gioia mia*. Your parents overreacted. Albert Einstein and some very famous people were also dyslexic,' Vitale fielded casually.

They boarded a private jet and as Zara settled into a cream leather seat in the cabin she was thinking once again about how very little she knew about the man she had married. 'I had no idea that you owned your own plane,' she confided.

'I travel a lot. It speeds up my schedule and ensures that I can move quickly in a crisis—'

'Where are we heading?' she prompted.

'It's a surprise, hopefully one which will please you.'

Lunch was served. After several sleepless nights spent worrying about the unknowns in her future, Zara was too exhausted to do more than pick at the food on her plate. Finally she pushed the plate away and closed her heavy eyes to rest them. That was the last thing she registered until the jet landed and Vitale shook her shoulder to rouse her from a deep sleep.

She was torn between pain and pleasure while he drove her through the Tuscan hills, for although she loved the Italian landscape she could not forget how much he had hurt her on her last visit.

'Isn't this the road we took to the Palazzo Barigo?' she pressed at one point.

'Sì.' His classic profile was taut, his response clipped.

When the car actually turned beneath the arched entrance to the palazzo, Zara turned with a frown to exclaim, 'What are we doing here?'

'You'll see.' Vitale parked at the front of the palazzo and, filled with curiosity, Zara scrambled out. Was he planning to introduce her to his uncle? Smoothing her dress down while wishing he had given her some warning of his intentions, she mounted the shallow flight of steps to the front door, which was already opening. She came to a sudden halt when she saw the domestic staff assembled in the marble hall, clearly waiting to greet them.

Joining her, Vitale curved a hand to her elbow and introductions were made. There was no sign of any member of the family and she was confused when a middle-aged manservant called Edmondo showed them into a spacious reception room where once again she expected to meet Vitale's relatives, only nobody awaited them there either.

'What on earth are we doing here?' she demanded of Vitale in a perplexed whisper. 'Is this where we're going to stay?'

'I own the palazzo,' Vitale told her flatly, breaking the news with the minimum possible fanfare.

CHAPTER NINE

VITALE's blunt confession hit Zara like a brick thrown at a glass window, shattering her composure. She recalled the tour of the gardens that he had said he had arranged. She remembered the gardener waving at him that same day and she turned pale before a flush of mortified pink mantled her cheekbones.

'Oh, my goodness, what an idiot I am!' she gasped, her temper rising hot and fast because she felt exceedingly foolish. 'But you told me this place belonged to your uncle—'

'No, I didn't. I only told you that I was staying here with my uncle and his family when your aunt worked on the garden—'

'Semantics—you *lied*!' Zara shot the furious accusation back at him. 'You're so tricky I'll never be able to trust a word you say!'

Vitale stood very still, reining back the aggression that her condemnation threatened to unleash. 'I bought the palazzo two years ago when my uncle decided to sell up but, while I have instigated repairs and maintained the property, I have not attempted to make personal use of the house until now,' he admitted without any expression at all.

He watched her, the daylight flooding through the tall windows burnishing her eye-catching hair and illuminating the fine lacework on her dress while enhancing the slender, striking elegance of her figure. He wondered when her pregnancy would start showing and experienced a glimmer of excitement at the prospect that shook him. But the awareness that her body would soon swell with visible proof of *his* baby turned him on hard and fast, no matter how fiercely he fought to repress the primitive reaction. Once again in her presence he was at the mercy of feelings and thoughts that were foreign to him and he hated it, craving the cool distance and self-discipline that were more familiar to him.

Zara settled furious lavender eyes on her bridegroom. 'Why not? If you bought the palazzo why haven't you used it?'

'I didn't feel comfortable here. When I was a teenager I stayed in this house during my term breaks and I have no good memories of those visits,' he admitted with a hard twist of his eloquent mouth.

'So what are we doing here?' Zara demanded baldly, still all at sea.

'You love the garden—I assumed that you might also like the house. It is a fine one.'

Zara was more confused than ever. An ancestral home was right off the grid of her scale of experience. To talk of it in terms of liking or disliking seemed positively cheeky. Yes, she had friends who inhabited such properties and she had occasionally stayed in them for the weekend but it had never occurred to her that she might one day actually live in one. 'Why did you buy a place this size if you don't even like it?'

'The palazzo has belonged to the Barigo family for centuries. I felt it was my duty to buy it and conserve it for the next generation.'

'But your name isn't Barigo…' Zara was still hopelessly at a loss.

'I have chosen not to claim the name but I am a Barigo.'

The penny of comprehension dropped noisily in Zara's head and she was embarrassed that it had taken her so long to make that leap in understanding. That was why he and his sister had had different surnames. They must have had different fathers. Evidently he was an illegitimate Barigo, born outside marriage and never properly acknowledged by the rest of the family. Yet he seemed so very much at ease against the grandeur of the great house, she mused. He had the education, the sophistication, the inborn classy assurance to look at home against such a splendid backdrop. He also had a level of worldly success and wealth that the most recent of the palazzo's owners had evidently lacked. Yet in spite of all that, deep down inside himself, Vitale had still not felt good enough to stay in the palazzo he owned and relax there and that disturbing truth twisted inside Zara's heart like a knifepoint turning.

'If you buy a house, you should use it,' Zara told him squarely. 'You seem to have a lot of staff employed here and you maintain it. My aunt used to say that a house that isn't lived in loses its heart.'

'I'm not sure that the Palazzo Barigo ever had a heart,' Vitale contended wryly. 'My sister grew up here. It was different for her. This was her home until her father died and my uncle inherited.'

'Why didn't your sister inherit?'

'The palazzo only goes to the men in the family. Loredana got the money instead,' he explained.

'So, why did you have to buy it to get it?' Zara pressed curiously. 'Because you're illegitimate?'

'I'm *not* illegitimate…it's too complicated to get into now,' Vitale countered with a dismissive shrug of a broad shoulder.

He didn't want to talk about his background and the shutters came back down. He was shutting her out because he didn't want to tell her any more. But these surroundings, his evidently troubled early life and what had happened to him since then were the key to Vitale's complex personality. Just then she recalled the strange scarring on his back and wondered once again what had caused it. At the same time, Zara was mystified by the depth of her longing to understand what drove Vitale Roccanti. Once she had thought he was a cold, callous guy focused purely on revenge, but the tiny seed of life inside her womb had steamrollered over that conviction and triumphed. As had her own personal safety, she conceded, recalling how he had brought her father to her door.

'Let's take a look at the house,' she responded lightly,

eager to distract him from the bad memories that he had mentioned.

'You're hardly dressed for a grand tour—'

'I can change.'

'I was rather looking forward to taking that dress off for you, *cara mia*,' Vitale admitted with a charismatic smile playing attractively at the corners of his beautifully shaped mouth.

'Well, you're going to have to help me get out of it. Getting into it was a two-person job,' Zara confided, thinking of the complex lacing that ran down her spine. 'I would never have managed without Bee's help this morning.'

As they reached the imposing marble staircase Edmondo appeared to show them the way and set off ahead of them at a stately pace that very nearly gave Zara a bout of irreverent giggles. Her dancing eyes meeting Vitale's in shared amusement, she had to swallow hard. The massive bedroom Edmondo displayed for their benefit was full of such extravagantly gilded furniture, embroidered, tasselled and fringed drapes and grandeur that Zara thought it would have been better suited to a reigning monarch. But there was no mistake because their luggage awaited them beside a pair of monumentally vast mirrored wardrobes.

'Wow…' she framed in a fading voice once they were alone again, unable to even imagine sleeping in that huge bed festooned in crimson drapes falling from a giant ceiling-mounted golden crown.

'What do you really think?' Vitale prompted as she bent to open her case and extract a change of clothing.

'It's hideous but I'm sure the antiques are worth a fortune and very historic,' she added in a rush, recognising that she might just have been tactless in the extreme.

'We could put them in storage and refurnish. It's not my style either,' Vitale admitted, stepping behind her to unknot the satin lacing closing the back of her dress. 'But Edmondo is a stickler for tradition and this is where the owner of the palazzo has always slept.'

'My goodness, your predecessors must've enjoyed their pomp and ceremony.' Zara shivered a little as cooler air brushed her bare shoulder blades and the fitted bodice of her gown loosened and fell forward. 'While you're a dab hand at unlacing.'

Vitale bent his head and pressed his lips to the tender side of her throat where a tiny pulse was going crazy. Lingering to enjoy her smooth, delicately perfumed skin, he used his mouth to nuzzle the soft skin there. His attention to that particular spot was unbearably arousing and a helpless gasp was wrenched from her as streamers of fire shot to every erotic zone she possessed. Stretching back against him for support, she caught her reflection in one of the wardrobe mirrors. She looked wanton, possessed, her hair shimmering round her shoulders, her face turned up eagerly to his, her breasts swelling and straining over the slightly too small cups of her lace strapless bra.

'I look like a shameless hussy,' she cried in embarrassment, her hands reaching down to pull up her dress again.

'Shameless works a treat for me, *angelina mia*,'

Vitale told her, his hands releasing her hold from the fabric so that her gown slid off her hips and down to her ankles. He lifted her out of the entangling folds and brought her down on the bed where he studied her scantily clad body with smouldering appreciation. 'You look gorgeous, Signora Roccanti.'

Self-conscious heat seemed to flood Zara from her head to her toes. She felt as though she were burning up inside her skin while her nipples tingled into straining buds and the tender flesh at the heart of her tingled with awareness. Dispensing with his tie, his waistcoat and his jacket and shoes, he lay down beside her, eyes full of anticipation. Zara propped herself up on her elbows, secure in his admiration, satisfied that she was both wanted and desired. He captured her lips with devastatingly erotic urgency so that even before he eased a small breast free of the bra her breath was parting her lips in rapid, uneven gasps. He rubbed the stiff rosy peak between thumb and forefinger and then dropped his mouth there to tease the throbbing tip with his lips and his tongue. As he simultaneously stroked the band of taut silk fabric stretched between her legs and felt the dampness there he groaned out loud. 'I've been fantasising about this moment for weeks,' he confided in a roughened undertone.

Only as he undid her bra to remove it did he spot the small blue badge she had attached to it. 'What's this?' he questioned.

'The something blue from the wedding luck rhyme and to remind me of my brother. He got it at school for playing rugby or something,' she muttered vaguely.

'I didn't even know you had a brother.'

'Tom was my twin. But he died in a car crash two years ago.' Flinching from her poignant recollections, she let her fingers delve into his tousled black hair to draw his mouth back to hers again and when he took her invitation to stop talking and kiss her it was so exhilarating that all sad memories left her head.

Her bra melted away, quickly followed by her panties. Vitale reared back on his knees to shed his remaining garments with a great deal more haste than cool. She revelled in his impatience, his eagerness to make love to her.

'I wanted this to be slow and perfect, unlike the last time,' Vitale admitted in a tone of frustration.

'Human beings don't do perfect,' she quipped, lifting a slender hand to run her fingertips gently down his cheek. 'And I don't expect it.'

'But you should,' Vitale informed her, eyes welded to her like padlocks.

With a gentle laugh of disagreement she arched her back below the hands curving to the pert swell of her sensitised breasts.

'Is it my imagination or is there more of you than there was a few weeks ago?' he teased.

'Falling pregnant does have some advantages,' she told him seductively. 'Alcohol may not be a good idea but I'm getting very bosomy indeed.'

Vitale laughed and kissed her breathless. She quivered as he found her clitoris with the ball of his thumb and pleasured her, gently delving and stroking until she moaned in helpless response to his stimulation. She was twisting and turning, her hips rising long before he rose over her and eased into her honeyed depths in a long deep thrust that sent a wave of excitement currenting through her.

'Don't stop,' she told him at an ecstatic peak of pleasure when it was a challenge to even find her voice.

She couldn't lie still as his fluid movements grew more insistent, more passionate and the intolerable tightness and tension within her gathered with every heartbeat and then exploded into an earthshaking climax. She hit that high with a startled cry of delight that she muffled by burying her mouth in a strong brown shoulder. She was as weak as a kitten once the tingling ripples of rapture had slowly coursed away from her again.

'I don't want to stroke your ego but that…*that* was perfect,' Zara whispered shakily, her hands sliding down from his shoulders to his back and instinctively massaging the roughened skin there with a gentle touch. 'What happened to you?' she asked him abruptly.

His muscles jerked taut below her fingers, and he stared down at her with bleak eyes. 'I was beaten, tortured as a child by my stepfather. He went to prison for it.'

A surge of horror swiftly followed by tears of sympathy flooded Zara's eyes. She lowered her lashes before he could see and when he tried to pull away from her, she held on tight to him. 'I thought I'd bottomed out in the parenting stakes,' she remarked tightly. 'But obviously you did a lot worse.'

Vitale realised that it would be more dignified to

stop fighting the comforting hug being forced on him. There was a ghastly moment when he just didn't know how to respond and he froze in her arms. She was always petting the rabbit, he reminded himself grimly; affectionate gestures were second nature to the woman he had married. He would have to learn how to handle them. He dropped a brief and awkward kiss on her brow, watching in dismay as a single tear inched down her flushed cheek on his behalf. 'We may not have done well in the parent lottery but that won't stop us being amazing parents,' he stated with powerful conviction. 'I'm sure we both know what *not* to do with our child.'

Zara thought of the mess that had been made of his back, the pain he must have endured and the despair he must have felt until he was removed from that cruelly abusive environment and she wanted to weep, but she had to confine herself to a subtle sniff or two and a comparatively modest hug. He saw hope in the future and refused to dwell on past suffering, she recognised with respect. Their marriage truly did have all the potential it needed to survive.

'My mother, Paola, married a wealthy businessman when she was eighteen. His name was Carlo Barigo and he was twenty years older,' Vitale said in a charged undertone, finally caving in and telling Zara the story that she had longed to hear since the day of her arrival as a bride at the palazzo.

Unfortunately prising that tale out of a male as reserved as Vitale was had taken determination and spot-on timing even from a wife of almost eight weeks' standing. At that instant, Vitale was at his most relaxed in a post-sex sprawl in the tangled sheets of their bed and her fingers were gently engaged in smoothing through his black hair.

'Go on,' she encouraged, quick to react to a hint of hesitation.

'Loredana was born within the first year of the marriage and within five years Paola was taking advantage of the fact that her husband was often away on business. She made friends with the wrong people, got into drink and drugs and started an affair. The marriage broke down. Carlo threw her out and her parents turned their back on her. She had never worked in her life and she was pregnant so she moved in with her lover—'

'The guy who beat you?' Zara cut in with a frown.

'*Sì*...he was a drug dealer to the rich. He married her because he assumed the divorce settlement would be huge—it was not. He also assumed that the child she was expecting was his.'

'That was you,' she guessed.

'I was Carlo Barigo's legitimate son but Paola lied and said I wasn't because my father had already deprived her of her daughter and she didn't want to lose me as well,' Vitale explained curtly. 'That was also my stepfather's excuse for beating me—that I wasn't his kid—but the truth was he got off on brutality.'

'Didn't your mother try to stop him?'

'By that stage all she cared about was her next fix.'

'There must have been someone who cared,' Zara said painfully.

'Not until Loredana decided that she wanted to meet

her mother after Carlo Barigo died. But when my sister visited us Paola was out of her head on drugs and Loredana got to know me instead. When she saw my bruises she notified the authorities of her suspicions. I went into the foster system and my stepfather eventually went to prison. I owe my life to Loredana's intervention,' he breathed heavily. 'I was eleven when she became my guardian. I went to boarding school while she worked as a model.'

For the first time she understood the foundation of his deep attachment to his late sister and her memory. Although his mother had failed him Loredana had saved him from a life of abuse.

Zara gazed down at his strong profile, so beautiful, so strong and yet so damaged, she conceded painfully. 'So how did you manage to visit this house as a teenager?'

'Loredana was an heiress, *gioia mia*. My uncle encouraged her to continue treating the palazzo like her home because he hoped that she would marry one of his sons and bring her money back into the family. That's why she was allowed to bring me here. It was that or leave me at school all the year round,' he proffered with a rueful sigh. 'My sister accepted me just as I was and I *was* rough round the edges. It never occurred to her that her snobbish cousins would be outraged to have a drug dealer and a junkie's son forced on them as a guest.'

Her brow furrowed. 'But that's not who you were.'

'It's what they believed. My cousins used to drag me out of bed in the middle of the night and thump and kick me and, thanks to their desire to ensure that I didn't get too big for my boots, I learned that my mother was selling her body to survive.'

Zara was pale. 'I bet you didn't even tell your sister what was happening.'

'Of course I didn't. I idolised her. She thought I was being treated to a slice of the family life she couldn't give me.' His mouth quirked. 'She was very trusting that way, always thought the best of everyone—'

'What age were you when she died?'

'Thirteen.'

'And how did you find out who your father really was?'

Vitale grimaced. 'The DNA testing that had to be done to identify Loredana's body revealed that we were full siblings. I chose to keep that news to myself. She hadn't changed her will to include me but a portion of her estate was set aside by the courts to cover my educational and living costs. My uncle got the rest and, being conscious of what people might think, he insisted that I continue to spend my term breaks at the palazzo.'

'Your sister was part of your life for such a short time.' Zara could only imagine how painful that loss must have been for a boy who had never known love and caring from any other source. It was even sadder that their true relationship had only been discovered after his sister had drowned.

'She first met your father here at the palazzo,' Vitale volunteered abruptly, his tone harsh. 'The grounds were being used for a fashion shoot and your aunt, Edith, was still working on her design. Loredana was modelling and your father flew in to see your aunt and he was invited to stay to dinner.'

'Oh,' Zara pronounced, it being her turn to pull a face, for she did not wish to tackle that controversial issue again at that moment for she was too well aware that, had her father been a braver man, Loredana might have survived the sinking of the yacht. 'Let's not discuss that now. Give me one positive thought about the palazzo, Vitale.'

'That is *so* childish, *cara mia*,' he groaned, looking at her in reproach.

'It's not...you can be very prone to taking a negative stance.'

A rueful smile chased the tension from his well-shaped mouth and he threw his untidy dark head back on the pillow. As dark, bronzed and glossy as a tiger at rest, he looked incredibly handsome. 'I commissioned the temple above the lake as a tribute to Loredana. The top of that hill was her favourite place—'

'That was a cheat thought...a sort of positive and negative together,' Zara censured.

'I won't need to commission anything to remember you,' Vitale teased with sudden amusement. 'Everywhere I look you've made your mark on this household.'

The huge pieces of gilded furniture had already gone into storage in favour of contemporary pieces in oak, which looked surprisingly well against the silk-panelled walls. Welcoming seating had arrived along with cushions, throws, unusual pieces of pottery and flower arrangements to illuminate dark corners and add comfort and character. Edmondo, who thoroughly approved of such nest-building instincts, had cheerfully described the new mistress of the palazzo to her husband as a 'force of nature'.

'You don't need to remember me,' Zara countered. 'I'm not going anywhere.'

His attention suddenly fell on the little jewelled enamel clock by her side of the bed and he stiffened and sat up in an abrupt movement. 'I didn't realise it was almost six!'

Within ten seconds of that exclamation, Vitale had vacated the bed and the shower was running in the adjoining bathroom. Zara lay on in the bed as stiff as a wooden plank while her mind whirled off on a wheel of frantic resentful activity. Sadly, she knew exactly why Vitale was in such a hurry. Well, at least she knew and she didn't know…

Once again, after all, it was a Friday night and every Friday night for the past five weeks Vitale had religiously gone out alone and not returned home until around two in the morning. He would only say that he visited a longstanding female 'friend', who lived near Florence, for dinner and if Zara tried to extract any more details from him he became irritable and broodingly silent. She suspected and had asked if that female friend was living in the villa for which she had done the garden plan but, rather tellingly, he had ignored the question.

'You must learn to trust me. You may be my wife but that doesn't mean I have to tell you *everything*!' he had argued without hesitation the previous week.

But Zara thought marriage should mean exactly that even though she had backed off from the looming threat of a row for the sake of peace. When Vitale returned to the palazzo tomorrow, however, she already knew that he would be grim and distant and that it would probably be at least forty-eight hours before he so much as touched her again. His Friday nights away from her, it seemed, did not put him in a good mood.

Was he spending that time placating another woman who mattered to him? A woman he had reluctantly set aside so that he could marry Zara because she had fallen pregnant? It was Zara's worst fear but what else could explain his tense, troubled attitude in the aftermath of those evenings? Vitale was betraying every sign of a man being torn between opposing loyalties.

It had to be admitted, though, that his mysterious Friday outings were the one and only storm cloud in Zara's blue sky and at first she had not been at all concerned when he left her to her own company one evening during the week. Her concern had grown only in proportion to his reticence. She did not like secrets and did not feel she could sit back and quietly allow him to maintain his secrecy.

Yet at the same time she had lived in Tuscany with Vitale for eight long weeks and had during that period discovered a happiness and a sense of security that was wonderfully new and precious to her. He had devoted the first three weeks of their marriage entirely to her, but after that point had had to return to the bank and his travels abroad. While he was away she had flown back to London on several occasions to catch up with business at Blooming Perfect and see clients.

Round her neck she wore a teardrop diamond pendant on a chain that Vitale hated her to take off. He had said the flash of the diamond in sunlight reminded him of her hair and her luminous smile. He had said loads and loads of romantic flattering stuff like that, words that she cherished, compliments that she took out and analysed whenever she was on her own or worried about the depth of his commitment to her and their marriage. He was very generous, had bought her innumerable gifts, everything from jewellery to flowers and artworks to pieces of furniture he thought she might like. Even more impressive he had also quietly engaged a speech-language specialist to visit weekly and help Zara overcome the problems caused by her dyslexia. She was already able to read more easily. Even Fluffy had benefited from Zara's move to Italy, having acquired more toys than even the most spoilt bunny could play with.

Vitale had become Zara's whole world without her even noticing it until she began to panic on Friday nights, worry about where he was and who he was with, and it made her realise her heart was more vulnerable than she had ever really appreciated. She was hopelessly in love with the guy she had married and to whom she had foolishly suggested a three-month-long trial marriage. Three months? Seriously, what sort of a stupid idea had that been? She already knew that she would not willingly give Vitale up after even a thousand months. What would she say at the end of the trial period if he was the one who turned round and jumped through that escape hatch she had handily provided to ask for *his* freedom back? It was a prospect that made her blood run cold.

She didn't know when she had fallen for Vitale or when she had first overcome that bad beginning when he had set her up for the paparazzi. But she was crazy about him and she really did understand that she had landed herself an extremely passionate, 'all or nothing' guy, who had switched his original allegiance to his sister's memory to their child instead. At heart she really did grasp what motivated Vitale more strongly than any other factor.

And what did inspire him was his movingly strong concept of what a man owed to his family. Her pregnancy had shot her right up the pecking order in his mind and brought her out at the top of the pile. She was carrying his baby, she was his wife and he really did treat her as though she was something incredibly precious. It touched her to the heart that even after the horrific experiences he had endured as a child he could still set such a very high value on the importance of family.

His cell phone rang and he emerged from the bathroom, a towel anchored precariously round his lean hips, to answer it. He frowned, thrust long impatient fingers through his damp black hair, spiking it up, and spoke in fluid Italian for several minutes, clearly issuing instructions. Setting the phone down again, he glanced at her. 'I'm afraid I have to fly to Bahrain this evening to meet a major investor. I won't be home until late tomorrow.'

As he broke the news Zara found herself smiling. If he had to be in Bahrain he couldn't also be dining somewhere near Florence with his unknown female friend. But if he didn't make it there this week he would presumably make it there at a later date. He walked over to the window and made another call, his attractive accented drawl apologetic, gentle in tone. Zara knew in her bones that he was talking to another woman and it wounded her, plunging her straight back into her uneasy thoughts.

Exactly what did Vitale get up to on Friday nights? He was risking their relationship by maintaining such secrecy. Didn't that bother him? Did he think this woman was worth that risk? Was he keeping a mistress in that luxury villa? A mistress he needed more than he needed his pregnant wife? She had to know. Who was he protecting her from? Or was it that he was protecting another woman from her?

Suddenly, Zara was determined to satisfy some of the questions that Vitale had refused to answer. Once he had left for the airport, she would drive over to the villa, make the excuse that she had come to check on the garden and discover who lived there. She had to know, she *needed* to know, and tough if he didn't like it when he found out that she'd gone behind his back to satisfy her curiosity…

CHAPTER TEN

THE local landscaping firm hired by Vitale to bring Zara's plan for the villa grounds to fruition had done an excellent job. A wide terrace girded by graceful trees and elegant shrubs had removed the old-fashioned formal aspect from the original frontage. Her heart beating very fast, Zara parked the car and approached the front door.

Whatever she discovered she would deal with it quietly and calmly, she reminded herself bracingly. She was ready to handle any eventuality. There would be no distasteful scene, no tears, certainly no recriminations. Hadn't she promised Vitale that before she married him? She was engaged in a trial marriage, which either one of them could walk away from without a guilt trip. If he *was* keeping another woman at the villa, if he *was* maintaining an extra-marital relationship, she had to set him free and get on with her life. Those far-reaching reflections were all very well, she reasoned in sudden dismay, as long as she didn't acknowledge that the very thought of having to live without Vitale, or raise her child without him, was terrifying.

It was a shock, therefore, while she hovered apprehensively on the doorstep, when without her even knocking to announce her presence the front door suddenly shot open and framed Giuseppina. Zara frowned when she recognised the housekeeper, who had looked after her and Vitale at the farmhouse where she had stayed several months earlier.

'Buona sera, Signora Roccanti,' Giuseppina greeted her with a welcoming smile and a further flood of Italian, which Zara did not understand.

With a display of enthusiasm that suggested that it was very unlikely that Vitale could be engaged in an improper extra-marital relationship with the villa occupant, Giuseppina ushered Zara into the hall. Quick light steps echoed across a tiled floor somewhere nearby and a woman appeared in the doorway.

She was an older woman, trim and not particularly tall with short silvery grey hair, anxious dark eyes and a heavily lined face. When she saw Zara she came to a sudden halt while Zara continued to stare, ensnared by a fleeting physical resemblance that took her very much by surprise.

'You must be Zara,' the woman breathed in accented English, her discomfiture unhidden. 'Did Vitale tell you about me? I made him promise that he would keep me a secret but I knew it would be difficult for him—'

'He didn't break his promise,' Zara admitted tautly, suddenly wishing she had stayed home, suddenly wishing she did not still suffer from that impulsive streak that invariably got her into trouble. 'I must apologise for dropping in without an invitation. I'm afraid I couldn't rest until I knew who was living here, who Vitale was seeing every Friday night…'

In the face of that explanation, the anxious expression on the other woman's face eased somewhat. '*Naturalmente…*of course. Come in—Giuseppina will make us English tea.' She spoke to the housekeeper in her own language before extending a hesitant hand. 'I am Paola Roccanti.'

'I thought you might be,' Zara almost whispered, shock still winging through her in embarrassing waves as she lightly touched that uncertain hand. 'Vitale has your eyes.'

Smiling as though that comment was a compliment, Paola took her into the lounge, smartly furnished now in contemporary style. 'I should have allowed Vitale to tell you I was here. I can see now that I put him in a difficult position. That was not my intention. I simply didn't want to embarrass you or him. I didn't want you to feel that you had to acknowledge me—'

'How could you embarrass me?' Zara asked in bewilderment. 'Why wouldn't I acknowledge you?'

Paola sighed. 'You're married to my son. You must know how badly I let him down as a child. Many people despise me for the life I have led and I understand how they feel. I've taken drugs, lived on the streets, I've been in prison for stealing to feed my addiction—'

'If Vitale wants to see you that is enough for me,' Zara broke in quietly, feeling that such revelations were none of her business.

'Since I came out of rehabilitation my son and I have been trying to get to know each other. It is not easy for either of us,' his mother confessed with a regret that she couldn't hide. 'It is hard for Vitale not to judge me and sometimes I remember things that make it almost impossible for me to face him.'

'I think it's good that both of you are trying, though,' Zara responded with tact as Giuseppina entered with a tray of tea.

Paola compressed her lips. 'Coming to terms with my past and facing up to the mistakes I made is part of my recovery process. I attend Narcotics Anonymous meetings regularly,' she explained. 'I have a good sponsor and Vitale has been very supportive as well.'

'That's good.' Still feeling awkward, Zara watched her companion pour the tea with a slightly trembling hand, her tension obvious.

'On Fridays we usually go for a meal and we talk, sometimes about difficult things…like my daughter, Loredana,' Paola continued quietly. 'I have no memory of her beyond the age of six or seven when I left my first husband, Carlo. She visited twice when she was grown up but I was in no condition to speak to her and I can't remember her—'

'Vitale told me…'

'You must know some of the bad things at least.' Paola's eyes were moist, her mouth tight with anxiety. 'He could have died when he was a child. I think he often wished he had when he was younger. I deprived him of his true father and his inheritance and yet he puts me in a house like this and takes me out to dine in fancy restaurants as if I was still the respectable young woman who married his father…the woman I was before I became an addict. He says I can be whoever I want to be now.'

'He's right. You can be,' Zara said gently, soothingly. It was impossible not to recognise how fragile Paola was and how weighed down she was with shame for her past mistakes. She found herself praying that the older woman did make it successfully through the recovery process and managed to stay off drugs.

Paola asked her about the garden and then offered to show it to her. Zara began to relax as they discussed the design and Vitale's mother asked for advice on what to plant in the empty borders behind the villa. Paola had already visited a garden centre nearby. Zara was quick to suggest that they should go back there together the following week and she agreed a date and time while hoping that Vitale would approve and not think her guilty of interference.

It was late afternoon the next day before Vitale returned to the palazzo. Dressed in a simple white sundress, Zara was arranging an armful of lavender in a fat crystal vase in the hall. He strode through the door and came to a halt, brilliant dark eyes locking to her tiny figure, picking up straight away on the troubled look she shot at him. Her pregnancy was becoming obvious now, a firm swell that made her dress sit out like a bell above her slender shapely legs.

'You can shout if you want,' Zara told him ruefully.

An ebony brow rose. 'Why would I shout?'

'I went to see your mother. I assumed you'd already know.'

'I did. Paola rang me as soon as you left the villa,'

Vitale confided with a wry smile. 'She likes you very much and thinks I did very well for myself, which I already knew—'

'But I went behind your back quite deliberately,' Zara pointed out guiltily, keen to ensure that he had grasped exactly what she had done. 'I just had to know where you went on Friday nights and who you were spending time with—'

'It was hell not telling you but I didn't want to spook Paola by forcing the issue. It took a lot of persuasion to get her to move into the villa. She's afraid of encroaching on our lives and of embarrassing us—'

'Are we that easily embarrassed?'

'I'm not, if you're not.' His sardonic mouth hardened. 'She lost thirty years of her life to drug abuse and she's made a huge effort to overcome her problems. I think she deserves a fresh start.'

'But you've found seeing her…difficult,' she selected the word uneasily.

'I didn't like the secrecy and it does feel strange being with her. I never knew her when I was a child and from the age of eleven until this year I had no contact with her, nor did I want any. We have a lot of ground to catch up but I've learned stuff from her that I'm grateful to have found out,' he admitted levelly, accompanying her up the marble staircase. 'Do you mind if I go for a shower? I feel like I've been travelling all day.'

'Not at all. What did you learn from Paola?' she probed curiously as he thrust wide the door of their bedroom.

'That my father kept a mistress throughout the whole

of their marriage.' Vitale raised a brow with expressive scorn. 'He only married my mother to have children and he didn't treat her well. It's not surprising that the marriage broke down or that she was suffering from such low self-esteem that she went off the rails.'

'But it was a tragedy for both you and her…and your sister as well,' Zara completed. 'How did your mother come back into your life again?'

'I was first approached on her behalf by a social worker several years ago but at the time I refused to have anything to do with her,' Vitale confided as he shrugged free of his jacket. 'Then I met you and I began to realise that human beings are more complicated than I used to appreciate.'

'What have I got to do with it?' Zara prompted with a frown.

'I used to be very black and white about situations. People, though, are rarely all good or all evil but often a mixture of both and we all make mistakes. After all, I made a big mistake targeting you to get at your father,' Vitale volunteered grimly. 'That was wrong.'

'I never thought I'd hear you admit that.' Zara curled up on the bed and looked at him expectantly. 'When did you reach that conclusion?'

Vitale dealt her a sardonically amused appraisal. 'There were quite a lot of helpful pointers after I met you, *angelina mia*. How about my discovery that you could get under my skin in the space of one weekend when I had already wrecked my chances with you? How about when you learned that you were pregnant and told me at the same time that you hated and distrusted me? Or even how about your need to impose a ridiculous three-month trial on our marriage so that you could get out of the commitment again if you had to? Do you think I'm so slow that I couldn't learn from those experiences?'

'It has never once crossed my mind that you might be slow—'

'But I was when it came to recognising and understanding my emotions,' Vitale interrupted, trailing his tie loose and tossing it aside. 'When I was a kid, it was safer to squash my feelings and get by without them because anything I felt only made me more vulnerable.'

'I can understand that,' Zara conceded, picking up the tie he had dropped on the floor and frowning at him.

'So I'm untidy,' he conceded with a flourish of one dismissive hand, well into his stride now with his explanation. 'As an adult I didn't recognise emotions for what they were, the same way as I didn't recognise what I felt for my mother until it was almost too late for me to get the chance to know her. By the time a priest who worked with Paola in rehab came to see me this year you were in my life and I was more willing to credit that I might not know everything there was to know and to listen to what he had to tell me.'

'I don't get my connection,' she admitted freely, draping the tie over the back of a chair in a manner that she hoped he would learn to copy.

'Well, once I fell in love with you it opened the floodgates to the whole shebang!' he pointed out mockingly. 'I mean, I've even learned to be reasonably fond of Fluffy now. Going from loving you to trying to understand my mother's need to make amends and be forgiven wasn't that difficult…'

Zara blinked and stared at him in disbelief, lavender eyes huge. 'You fell in love with me…*when*?'

A wicked grin flashed across his beautifully shaped mouth as he realised he had taken her by surprise. 'Oh, I think it probably happened that first weekend when I was playing at being the evil seducer and setting you up with the paparazzi. In fact, as I later appreciated, I was setting myself up for a fall. I didn't know I was in love back then, I just felt like you had taken over my brain because I couldn't get you out of my head, nor could I stay away from you.'

'So when did you decide it was love?'

'Slowly, *painfully*…' Vitale stressed ruefully, his face serious. 'When I'm with you I'm happy and secure. When I've been away from you and I'm coming home I'm downright ecstatic. Everything has more meaning when you're with me. Loving you has taught me how to relax, except when I'm worrying about you.'

'What have you got to worry about me for?'

'It's that naturally negative bent my thoughts suffer from,' Vitale confided ruefully, shedding his shirt. 'The more you mean to me, the more scared I am of losing you, and sometimes when I look at you I am terrified of what I feel—like when I came through the front door and saw you standing there with those purple things—'

'The lavender,' she slotted in.

'Whatever, *angelina mia*.' With a fluid shift of one hand he dismissed an irrelevant detail. 'You were standing there looking so beautiful and pleased to see me and yet worried and I had this moment of panic that something had happened, that something was wrong—'

'I was just worried that you would be annoyed at my having gone behind your back to see who was living in the villa.'

'No, I was touched by your compassion. You spent time with Paola. You didn't make her feel bad. You even invited her out—'

'She needs company,' Zara pointed out. 'It's no big deal.'

'It would be a very big deal to some women. There will be gossip, even scandal if Paola becomes a part of our lives. Some people will approve, others will not.'

'That doesn't matter to me. Let's see how things go,' Zara suggested, knowing that the older woman still had a long way to go as part of her recovery process and that the continuing success of her rehabilitation could not be taken for granted.

'She needs us to have faith in her—she's got nobody else.' Naked but for his boxer shorts, Vitale ran a knuckle gently down the side of Zara's face. 'But I've been hell to live with while this was going on, haven't I?'

'You were a little moody after seeing her.'

'And you don't like moody guys,' he reminded her with a grimace. 'It was tough at first. But although seeing Paola roused bad memories it also made me view my past in a more even light.'

'I really like the fact that you're making that effort for your mother,' Zara confided softly, her tender heart touched. 'It would have been easier for you to turn your back on her.'

'I think it's actually harder to hang onto the prejudices, as I did over Loredana.' Vitale compressed his handsome mouth. 'I will never like your father—he is not a pleasant man and he hurt you. But speaking to him about the night my sister drowned did show me that I was still thinking of that incident with the vengeful attitude of a teenager distraught over his sister's death.'

'Yes,' Zara agreed feelingly.

'Someone else isn't always to blame for the bad things that happen,' he acknowledged heavily. 'Although your father, in fact *both* your parents are very much to blame for your unhappy childhood. To have stood by and allowed you to be branded a liar at the age of ten to conceal your father's violence towards your mother and you was unforgivable. That was a huge betrayal of your trust.'

'I got over it.'

'And I don't think I will ever understand why you were still willing to marry Sergios Demonides just to cement a business deal and win your parents' approval.'

'It was very foolish but I had spent so many years craving their approval without ever getting it. I didn't have enough self-respect,' she admitted wryly. 'I had to come to Tuscany to realise that to marry a man I didn't love or care about was a very bad idea.'

'I had an identical moment of truth when I met you. You changed my outlook, *gioia mia*,' Vitale confided in a tone of immense appreciation. 'I didn't like emotions, didn't trust them, preferred not to get involved with anything or anybody that made me feel too much. But you taught me how much of a difference love could make to my life and then you taught me to want your love…'

Heaving a delighted sigh at that assurance, Zara rested a small hand on his shoulder. 'You know that three-month trial marriage I mentioned?'

'Don't I just?'

'I won't keep you in suspense,' Zara told him teasingly. 'I've decided to keep you for the long haul.'

The beginnings of a smile started to tug at the corners of Vitale's mouth. 'Finally she lets me off the hook.'

'I'm not convinced it did you any harm to be on that hook in the first place.' Zara mock-punched his shoulder. 'Sometimes you're far too sure of yourself. But I do love you,' she whispered, suddenly full of heartfelt emotion. 'I love you very much indeed.'

Vitale did not make it into the shower until much later that evening. In fact he didn't even make it out of the bedroom, for Edmondo was instructed to bring dinner to his employers upstairs. Having declared their love and revelled in the wonder of sharing the same feelings and opinions, Vitale and Zara made passionate love. Afterwards they lay on in bed for ages talking about the why and the how and the when of those first seeds of love until even Zara was satisfied that they had talked the topic to death.

It was definitely not hard for her to listen, however, to how enraged Vitale had felt on her behalf when he appreciated how little her parents valued her in comparison to the twin brother whom they assumed would have been perfect had he lived beyond his twentieth year. In turn, Vitale was hugely amused by the news that his kindness to Fluffy had alerted Zara to the idea that he might have a softer centre than his initial behaviour towards her might have suggested.

'So, I'm not on probation any longer,' Vitale commented with a hint of complacency.

'And how do you work that out?' Zara enquired, surveying him questioningly.

'You said you wanted me for the long haul.'

'Depends on your definition of long haul,' she teased.

'For ever and ever just like the fairy tales,' Vitale hastened to declare, spreading a large hand across the swell of her stomach and laughing in satisfaction as he felt the faint kick of the baby she carried. 'You and the baby both, *angelina mia*.'

'That's an ambition I'm happy to encourage,' Zara told him happily.

EPILOGUE

THREE years later, Zara watched her daughter, Donata, play in the bath in their London town house before scooping her out into a fleecy towel and dressing her little squirming body in her pjs. Her dark eyes were so like Vitale's that the little girl was very talented at wheedling things out of her mother.

'Daddy?' Donata demanded, first in Italian and then in English, demonstrating her bilingual language skill with aplomb.

'Later,' Zara promised, tucking the lively toddler into bed and reflecting that it would be the next morning before Donata saw the father she adored.

Vitale had spent the whole week in New York and, although Zara and occasionally their daughter sometimes travelled with him, she had taken advantage of his absence to catch up with plans needed for Blooming Perfect clients in both London and Tuscany. Business was booming in both countries to the extent that Zara had been forced to turn down work. Media interest and an award won for a garden she had designed for the Chelsea Flower Show had given her an even higher profile and resulted in a steady influx of clients. Rob had become a permanent employee and Zara had hired a junior designer to work under her in London.

Vitale's mother, Paola, had made it safely through her rehabilitation and as time went on had gained in confidence. Having undertaken training as a counsellor, Paola had recently found her feet in her new life by volunteering to work with other addicts. Vitale had also agreed to sponsor a charity for former addicts and their families. The older woman was now very much a part of Vitale and Zara's life and was a very fond grandparent—a fact that Zara was grateful for when her own parents had little to do with their lives.

While Vitale had managed to come to terms with his mother's malign influence on his childhood and had since established a more relaxed adult relationship with the older woman, little had occurred to improve Zara's relations with her parents in a similar way. Her father could not accept the fact that Vitale knew about the domestic violence that had cast such a shadow over Zara and her mother's life. In turn, Zara's mother, Ingrid, was too loyal to her husband to challenge his hostile attitude to their daughter and son-in-law.

Although Zara occasionally accompanied Vitale to social events in London that her parents also attended, and the two couples were always careful to speak for the sake of appearances, there was no true relationship beneath the social banter. Sometimes that hurt Zara a great deal more than she was willing to admit to Vitale. At the same time she did have reason to cherish some hope of a future improvement in relations because her mother made a point of phoning and asking her daughter when she would next be in London so that she could see Donata. Ingrid would then visit her daughter's home and play with her grandchild, but it was tacitly understood that those visits took place without Monty Blake's knowledge.

On the other hand Vitale had taught Zara that life by its very nature was imperfect and that nothing was to be gained from fighting the fact. Her sadness over her poor relationship with her parents was more than compensated for by the deep and happy bond of intimacy she had forged with her husband and child. Her confidence in his love made her smile when she wakened and smile again when she often fell asleep in the safe circle of his arms.

Their closeness had grown by leaps and bounds in the wake of Donata's birth. Vitale travelled less so that he could spend more time with his family. He was also very much a hands-on father, who enjoyed playing with his daughter and reading her stories. Zara could see that he was striving to give Donata the safe, loving childhood that fate had denied both of them and it touched her heart. On this particular evening, though, Zara gave her daughter less time to settle into bed than she usually did because it was the couple's third wedding anniversary and she and Vitale were going out to celebrate.

Zara donned an elegant blue designer dress that skimmed her slight curves and made the most of her height. As she did her make-up she was thinking of the announcement she had to make and smiling to herself, thinking of how different it would be this time from the last time when everything relating to her pregnancy had seemed so uncertain and scary.

Vitale strode through the door with all the impatience of a man who was always eager to see his wife after being away from her.

Zara appeared in the bathroom doorway. 'Vitale…' she murmured, skimming over him with helpless admiration, for she still marvelled over the fact that this gorgeous man was her husband and the father of her child.

'You look fantastic,' he breathed, his dark gaze running over the chic dress and lingering on that luminous smile echoed by the superb diamond pendant she always wore. 'Do we really have to go out?'

Her sultry mouth quirked. When Vitale was away from her for any appreciable length of time it took determination to get him out of the bedroom.

'I didn't go to all this trouble dressing up just to stay home—'

Vitale groaned, amusement and frustration etched in his lean dark face. 'I just want to grab you and unwrap you like a gift but I know this is a special occasion.'

'Our third anniversary,' Zara reminded him very seriously.

Her husband dug into his pocket and handed her a little box. 'A small mark of my appreciation and love…'

It was an eternity ring, composed of a hoop of beautiful diamonds that slotted onto her finger next to her wedding ring as though it had been made for that spot, which, as Vitale was very good at detail, it probably had been. 'It's gorgeous,' she carolled, pink with pleasure that he had made the effort to celebrate the occasion with such a present.

'I'm sorry, I'm going to have to wreck your make-up, *angelina mia*. I'm in the control of forces stronger than I am,' Vitale teased, closing his arms round her and claiming a passionate kiss.

And he did a lot more than wreck her make-up, for the passion that never failed them burst into being on contact with a strength that could not be denied and they happily gave way to pleasing each other in the oldest way of all. Afterwards, the dress was a little creased and the dinner reservation had to be moved to a later time.

They ate at their favourite Florentine restaurant by candlelight and somewhere between the first course and the final one Zara made her announcement and Vitale did not dare tell her that because she had refused the wine he had already guessed. Instead he gripped her hand and told her that the news she was carrying their second child was amazing, before adding quite truthfully that their three years together had been the happiest years of his life.

Meeting those dark golden eyes resting on her with adoration, Zara's gaze misted over. 'And mine…I love you so much.'

'And with every year that you are with me, I love you more, *angelina mia*.'

* * * * *

"DON'T YOU THINK you're being a tad dramatic?" he asked her in a wry voice.

"I'm not being dramatic," she defended herself. "Surely I should have some rights as a person, a human being, some say in my own fate, instead of having my future decided for me by my father. To endure marriage to a man who has simply agreed to marry me because he wants an heir, and to whom my father has virtually auctioned me off in exchange for a royal alliance."

"I should have thought such a marriage would suit you, Sophia. After all, it's well documented that your own chosen lifestyle involves something very similar, when it comes to bed hopping."

A body blow indeed, and one that drove the blood from Sophia's face and doubled the pain in her heart. It shouldn't matter what Ash thought of her. That was not part of her plan. But still his denunciation of her hurt, and it wasn't one she could defend herself against. Not without telling him far more than she wanted him to know.

"Then you thought wrong" was all she could permit herself to say. "That is not the kind of marriage I want. I can't bear the thought of this marriage." Her panic and fear were there in her voice; even she could hear it herself, so how much more obvious must it be to Ash?

She must try to stay calm. Not even to Ash could she truly explain the distaste, the loathing, the fear she had of being forced by law to give herself in a marriage bed in the most intimate way possible when… No, that was one secret that she must keep no matter what, just as she had already kept it for so long. "Please, Ash, I'm begging you for your help."

Will Ash discover Sophia's secret?
Find out in THE PRICE OF ROYAL DUTY
by
USA TODAY *bestselling author*
Penny Jordan

Book 1 of THE SANTINA CROWN *miniseries*
available May 2012 from Harlequin Presents®!

EXP0412